T0104799

CINDER RISING

CORLA RENN-DERIENZO

ARCHWAY
PUBLISHING

Archway Publishing books may be ordered through booksellers or by contacting:

Archway Publishing
1663 Liberty Drive
Bloomington, IN 47403
www.archwaypublishing.com
1 (888) 242-5904

ISBN: 978-1-4808-2626-7 (sc)
ISBN: 978-1-4808-2625-0 (e)

Library of Congress Control Number: 2015921379

Print information available on the last page.

Archway Publishing rev. date: 2/3/2016

This book is dedicated to my wonderfully amazing
and patient DeRienzo-Renn-Carr family...

Without your love and support,
none of this would have seen the light of day.

CONTENTS

Prologue 1
Chapter 1 7
Chapter 2 14
Chapter 3 18
Chapter 4 22
Chapter 5 27
Chapter 6 30
Chapter 7 33
Chapter 8 38
Chapter 9 40
Chapter 10 43
Chapter 11 46
Chapter 12 52
Chapter 13 61
Chapter 14 70
Chapter 15 75
Chapter 16 82
Chapter 17 86
Chapter 18 90
Chapter 19 94
Chapter 20 97
Chapter 21 99
Chapter 22 102
Chapter 23 104
Chapter 24 105
Chapter 25 108

PROLOGUE

Allanville, Pennsylvania
Twenty-Five Miles South of Philadelphia

It was half past eight on Saturday night, and Elaine sat at the bar. The place was attached to the Pleasant Cove Inn, a seedy establishment all on its own. Unfortunately, it was the only room she could afford. She had thought a better name for it was the Desperate and Raunchy Inn.

She looked around the room and let her gaze drift over a few lounge lizards and a group of truckers who were enjoying the little show the female patrons were currently putting on. Their skirts were so short Elaine questioned the point of even wearing one in the first place. Down at the end of the bar, a couple of old-timers were drowning their sorrows in the cheapest beer they could get their hands on.

Elaine stared down into her glass, her third gin and tonic of the night, and she was starting to feel it. While she was studying the liquid, she came to realize she would probably have enjoyed her buzz if not for the growing pit in her stomach. She hated the way it felt. She wanted to be anywhere but this godforsaken place, and yet this was her lot in life—never staying in once place for too long, hopping from one cheap, seedy area to another, always running.

Sometimes she wished she were like other thirty-two-year-old women: a husband, a handful of kids, a good job, and a little house in the suburbs. She thought that would be nice. But it was too dangerous now. She simply had to keep going, but where? She would constantly ask herself this.

Her head felt fuzzy, and her eyes in the bar mirror were glassy. Who the hell cared? She sure didn't—and neither did anyone else. She would not allow it. She finished off her drink. Just a few more, and she would be able to forget even her own name.

As Elaine set her glass back down on the bar, a man took up a stool beside her. The bartender was quick to make his way over to take the order of the stranger. *Ugh.* She could feel him staring at her. She fixed her eyes down on her empty glass, hoping he would hurry up and go with his drink, but it seemed that life wasn't going to be that kind to her. *When was it ever?*

"Hey there. Name's Bryce. Buy ya another drink?" he asked.

"No," Elaine stated flatly, keeping her eyes trained away from him. *Please go away,*

"Oh, come on, now. It's just one drink," he slurred.

"No," Elaine repeated.

"The least you can do is look at a fella when you turn him down, pretty lady," he said with a wily smile.

Elaine heaved a sigh and shut her eyes, thinking that if he knew much better, he'd be running for his life—that is, if he knew what was good for him. He was just going to continue to stare at her and wait for an answer, wasn't he? She sighed again, this time loudly enough for him to hear, and she reluctantly cocked her head up to look at him.

She noted his deep green eyes and sandy blond hair. From what she could tell, he wasn't much older than she was.

"That's better," he remarked. "Now, why don't you explain to me why you won't let me just buy you a drink?"

Elaine was annoyed, and the place between her brows dented as they furrowed in irritation. "Because I don't want another drink. Anyway, I was just on my way out." She tried to keep the venom out of her tone.

"I see." He tilted his head. "Do you have someone you're rushing off to then?"

"No, I'm just done drinking is all." Elaine slipped off of her stool and prepared to exit the bar.

"Then that would be a no to dinner?"

"I prefer to eat alone," Elaine interjected with a more irritated tone, turning her glance back at him as he persisted.

"A bit of a loner, aren't we?" He paid for his drink and carried it with him as he followed her.

"You could say that," she stated, searching for an out as her eyes found her goal. "But there are a couple of ladies over there who I'm sure would be more than happy to take you up on your offers." She pointed to the short-skirted lizards who were dancing as seductively as one so inebriated could to Quiet Riot's "Girls, Rock Your Boys."

Bryce barely gave them a once-over before he said, "I'm afraid none of those women are really my type."

"Oh." Elaine raised her brows, folding her arms tightly. "And what makes you think that I am?"

"Well," he started, taking a sip of his drink and putting his free hand on his hip, "you're quite beautiful, with long chestnut hair, which I'm quite crazy about, and you have the deepest brown eyes. Any man would love to get lost in those."

This made Elaine chuckle, even if only under her breath. "I do believe that I am much too old to fall for a pathetic line like that. Really, Bryce, I appreciate your effort, but I'm not interested, okay?"

His smile faltered slightly before he gave a nod. "Well, beautiful, if you change your mind, I'm staying in room 127—and you're free to join me."

With that, Elaine adjusted her shoulder bag and headed toward the ladies room. "Like I said, I'm just not interested. Now, if you'll excuse me." She hoped that he would be gone when she came back from the bathroom.

When she opened the door, she almost hurled. The stench of old urine hit her directly in the face. She closed the door behind her and squeezed her eyes shut, trying to steady herself and attempting to hold her breath. If there was one smell on the top of her hate list, it was piss.

Bryce didn't like it when women told him no, not one bit. He had a way with words, or rather, a way with keeping them in line. First, he would try the sweet and subtle approach. When that didn't work, he would simply take what he wanted. He wasn't about to let that bitch show him up and treat him like that, especially in front of other people. He was going to have to find a way to join her—and what a fun little party they would have. She had no idea what was in store for her, and she made the entirely wrong choice. He slammed his empty glass on the bar and wiped his mouth before staggering back to the bathroom.

He decided to relieve himself first. At the urinal, he thought out all of the things he would do to her. He would teach her a very, very important lesson.

As he zipped up and walked out, he was surprised at what, or better yet *who,* he found leaning up against the wall beside the pay phones.

"Well, hello, beautiful." He smirked. "Ready to party?" She just gave him a nod and a warm smile before pushing up off of the wall and taking his arm. Without a word, the two headed out the back.

Elaine hurriedly scrubbed her hands in the filthy hotel sink. She wasn't looking forward to having to walk past Bryce when she left the bar. She took a deep breath, although with the stench, it did nothing to calm her, and she walked out the door. When she went back out to where she could see the bar, she expected him to be waiting there for her, but he was gone. *Thank goodness for small favors.*

Elaine's stomach growled loudly. Bryce had gone on and on about food, and now she was starving. She hadn't eaten anything but a stale doughnut for breakfast. There wasn't a whole lot of money left in her front pocket, but it was enough to buy a burger, some beer-battered onion rings, and another gin and tonic.

The burger was one of the best she had tasted in a while, and the onion rings were fantastic. After shoveling her food down and finishing off her drink, she looked at her watch: a little past ten. *Time to head back,* she thought.

She made her way to the exit and stepped out into the crisp Pennsylvania air. Elaine stumbled slightly; that last drink had not been the best idea. She stopped, dug her room key out of her bag, and slowly made her way up the concrete steps to her room on the second floor. Her fingers gripped the metal handrail. She desperately needed a good night's rest. In the morning, she would try to find some sort of temporary work to earn some more money so she could continue on to parts unknown.

"Yes," she hissed with a slur as she had conquered the stairs. "Just a few more steps. Easy there, girl. Ah, here we are, ol' girl."

It took her a few minutes to steady her hand to the point where she could successfully get the room key into the lock.

"Damn thing," she slurred. "Why can't this place leap into the new millennium and just go with key cards?"

When she unlocked the door after what felt like forever, she pushed it open and slung her bag onto the chair beside the door. When she slapped the lights on, what she saw chilled her to the very core.

Her motel room was coated in blood; it was splattered, smeared, and pooled everywhere. Bryce was on the filthy aqua shag carpeting; his throat had been slashed clean across and back all the way up to each ear. The cut was so deep that his head looked like it would topple off with the smallest movement.

Elaine grabbed her stomach and began retching and heaving on the carpet. She stumbled with disbelief and fell into her vomit. "No! No! No! Damn you!" she cried out, scrambling to clamp her hands over his wound with some sort of delusional idea that it would bring him back to life. His green eyes that had been smiling at her so persistently earlier were now cold and lifeless. His sandy brown mop was nearly completely red and matted with his blood.

"Jesus, why? Why did you have to talk to me?" She grasped a fistful of her hair before throwing her hands down in frustration. "God, I'm so, so sorry." She dropped her head to her blood-covered hands and began to cry hysterically. Reeling at the smell, she stumbled to her feet. "Have to … get out." Elaine fell again and crawled toward the bathroom. "Get out … have to … not again. I can't. Not again." She rocked herself against the wall before spotting the towel on the bar and yanking it down, furiously trying to wipe the blood and vomit from her clothing.

She started to retch again and made it to the toilet before it felt like her stomach was trying to claw its way out of her throat with its contents. Sweat beaded off her forehead, and she wiped her face with her hand before she dragged herself back up to the sink to wash her face. She gasped when she looked up at her reflection and noticed the message left for her in the blood of the man in her room: *Bad Man Bad Man Had To Die.*

Elaine clutched the sides of the sink and squeezed her eyes shut, trying to breathe calmly. *All right, Elaine. Think think think. You need to get the hell out of here. Get away.* She grasped her head for the ache that was quickly working its way to relentless migraine. She calmly walked out of the bathroom and stepped over Bryce, careful not to touch any part of him. Feeling weak, she grabbed her bag and dug out the keys to her Ford pickup. The migraine was making it hard to concentrate. All she had to do was get down to the truck and drive as far away as she could get.

Her head was pounding, and her eyes stung badly. She desperately needed to lie down and rest, but she knew there was no time for that. She would just have to get herself out of there and celebrate with resting. Still covered in blood and vomit, she headed toward the stairs, not realizing she was leaving a trail of bloody footprints behind her. She had nearly forgotten where she had parked, which almost sent her into a deeper state of panic. She spotted it a few yards away from the stairs, but it looked hundreds of miles away.

The manager's wife came outside to light a cigarette and spotted Elaine. She hurried over to Elaine and said, "My dear, are you hurt? Do you need help?"

Elaine knew that someone was talking to her, but she couldn't concentrate enough to understand what the woman was saying. Elaine tried to shake her head, but the motion caused her to collapse to her knees.

The woman knelt behind her. "Good heavens! You wait here. I'll run and get help. Don't move." The woman ran back toward the office.

Elaine knew she couldn't stay there any longer. She needed to get to her truck before the woman came back. There was no time to waste. She pulled herself up and steadied herself against her truck. If she mustered all her energy, she would be able to do this. Everything was a blur as she attempted to focus on the door handle. She could hear sirens in the distance, which was the downside of a small town. She was thankful that she had forgotten to lock her truck and climbed in through the passenger's side, pulling the door behind her, but she could not get up enough strength to start the engine. Her head fell to the seat, and she closed her eyes. Her migraine pounded against her brain, and she passed out as the sirens got closer.

She awoke to the pounding of a fist on her window and the shouting of a figure outside the vehicle. Her head was in so much pain. Everything was going by in a blur. A stretcher and the inside of an ambulance were the last things she made out. She heard a woman say there was a dead man in one of the rooms.

It's a bad dream, just a bad dream, she thought.

The ambulance pulled out of the motel parking lot.

CHAPTER 1

Willow Tree Asylum
One Year Later

Elaine looked out at the beautifully tranquil pond, wondering how it ever got this far. Her life was not supposed to get this bad, and it was never supposed to be this way—not even close. She turned over her journal, running her fingers over the binding. The doctor told her that keeping a log of her thoughts was supposed to be good therapy. She flipped the book open and picked up her pen.

I need to put down my story so that someday people will understand that I'm not crazy, that bad things have happened, and I was doing everything in my power to stop them. How do you fight something created out of your own anger and hurt?

My story begins in my younger years, when I was only four years old, and the first time that I met ... her. She came to me first when I was in the middle of a nightmare. She was the most terrifying and intriguing thing I had ever seen. When we were small, we all had that fear of the unseen monsters that lived under our beds or the creatures that hid in the dark closet, but mine were not dispelled by my mother coming into the room and turning on the lights. This scary entity came to me night after night. She was skinny as a rail, and her skin was an unhealthy gray. She wore a long, dingy blue dress that fell off of her weak, bony frame. Her hair was wiry and long, black as a shadow, just like her big, empty eyes. Her teeth were jagged, and her tongue was missing. She would do terrible, terrible things, but I couldn't help feeling like she needed me— and that I needed her in return. Both of us were so lonely and afraid. I affectionately gave her the name Cinder, my demented opposite of Cinderella. For many years, we would secretly play together—and even though she couldn't speak to me, I always knew what she wanted and what she was about to do.

Elaine was about to finish up her entry for the day when the nurse came over to her side.

"Elaine, it looks like it's going to start raining. Why don't we go in for a while, okay?"

"Okay, Nurse Hadler. I was just finishing up here anyway." Elaine sat up and tapped her journal.

"I see you started your journal. That's really great, Elaine." Nurse Hadler smiled.

"Well, I know it's supposed to help if I write things down."

"Come on. Let's go inside before we both end up a couple of drowned rats." Nurse Hadler chuckled before leading Elaine back inside the hospital.

When they were inside, Elaine moved to her small room.

Sarah was sitting on the edge of her bed.

Elaine, wanting a little time to zone out before her session with Dr. Katz, flopped back onto the bed, listening to Sarah kick the bottom of her bed. She always did that when she wanted Elaine's attention. Sarah was holding her old stuffed dog, which she had named Tobbie. He was from her childhood, and she would not separate from him.

Both women were thirty-three years old. Sarah had stringy red hair, and her face and body were peppered with freckles, despite her incredibly pale complexion. She had been at the institution since she was nine years old. Her entire family perished in a tragic house fire: her parents, her older brother, and her older sister. While her family slept, Sarah started the fire and went out into the backyard. Her neighbors saw the fire and called 911.

When the police and the fire department arrived, Sarah was sitting on the lap of one of the female neighbors, clutching Tobbie to her chest. When she was questioned about the fire, she gave an angelic smile and stated, "Oh, yes, they are fried to a crisp. Crackle, crackle, crackle." The authorities thought witnessing the culprit setting the house ablaze had traumatized Sarah, but she was adamant that she had started the fire all on her own.

Sarah was kicking her heels harder against the bed.

Elaine heaved a breathless sigh and turned her head. "What is it, Sarah?" she asked with a smile.

"Did I tell you that Dr. Katz said I can have any kind of cake I want for my birthday?" Sarah was beaming.

"Yes, you did tell me. Have you decided which kind yet?"

"No. Not yet anyways. I'm thinking chocolate. It's been forever since I had chocolate. The last time I can remember is when Momma bought me a candy bar at the drugstore." Sarah tilted her eyes down at her shoes and lowered her voice. "Sometimes I really miss them. I wonder how heaven is. I wonder if they can see me. Elaine, do you think they can see me?"

"I'm not sure." Elaine let her neck relax. "But I'm sure that they miss you too."

Sarah lifted her head and smiled. "You really think so? Sometimes I miss Momma's pancakes and the way Daddy always smelled like English Leather. Bobby sometimes let me go with him to Dairy Queen, and Rebecca rolled my hair up in curlers on Saturday nights so that it would be cute for church."

Elaine's heart truly went out to Sarah. She smiled and said, "Sarah, I think that chocolate is a great choice for your birthday." Sarah bounced off of the bed and tenderly placed Tobbie on her pillow before she went off to the television room with the other patients.

Elaine was attempting to zone out when Nurse Hadler came trotting into the room, informing her that Dr. Katz wouldn't be able to see her until after lunchtime. Elaine nodded and changed into a pair of blue sweatpants and a white T-shirt. She threw her long hair up into a ponytail and went to the dining hall to join the others for lunch.

When she got into the dining hall, Sarah was sitting with Joan, Miles, and Phoebe. "Come, Elaine! Sit with us!" Sarah shouted from across the room. "Please?"

Elaine sat next to Joan and listened as Sarah went on and on about her birthday.

Miles practically hung on her every word. He had been an aspiring law student until he shot his fiancée during an argument.

Joan was in her fifties and had been institutionalized a little more than five years earlier when her bipolar disorder became too much for her life as a schoolteacher.

Phoebe's life was filled with every kind of abuse in the book. Up until her parents were killed in a car accident, they had kept her in the basement of their home. This made up the first fifteen years of her life, and the police recovered her during a wellness check the neighbors requested. She did not know that her parents had died. At eighteen, Phoebe was the youngest in the group. She seemed to thrive in asylum life since she needed her every move to be explained to her in detail.

Elaine sometimes entertained the group with stories of her travels around the country, omitting any of the less pleasant parts. She always tossed a happy spin on the end of everything.

As they ate their roasted chicken and mashed potatoes, Sarah suggested that they all watch *Gone With the Wind* after lunch—just as they had at least three times that week. It was Sarah's favorite movie. Joan and Miles would have fun mouthing the words of Scarlett and Rhett, which kept Sarah thoroughly entertained. Elaine slept on her edge of the couch.

"That sounds like a great idea, Sarah," Elaine said. "I will have to join up with you guys later. I have a session with Dr. Katz."

"Okay," Sarah said with a nod.

After she finished eating, Elaine went to her appointment with the doctor.

"Good afternoon, Elaine. How are you feeling today?"

"I'm doing all right, Dr. Katz. I actually started writing in that journal today."

"That is a very positive first step, Elaine. I know that writing your thoughts and feelings down can be a very freeing experience." He set his clipboard down and folded his hands over it. "You've been here for a whole year now, and you know that the court order dictates that I send them an annual report of your progress."

Elaine sat up. "Yes, I remember. He wants to see if I've come to grips with what happened, right?"

"That's right. But even though you've been here for so long and made such positive progress, we have yet to talk about Bryce Freeman and the night you were arrested."

Elaine started to feel that sinking feeling in her stomach again. She never wanted to think about that night again—let alone talk about it.

At the asylum, things had begun to even out for her. She was starting to feel normal again, strange as she thought it was sometimes. She'd never had people who cared about her that way anywhere else she'd been. Elaine wanted to stay for as long as she could. She knew that while she was there, everyone else was safe too. Nobody was going to be hurt because of her.

"Dr. Katz, I really don't have anything to say on the matter."

"Elaine, the staff and I feel like you have a real potential to recover and grow from this. There are many patients I see throughout the week with no hope for that opportunity. With a little bit of hard work, you could even be released, but we can't let that happen if you don't talk about this. I read the case file. I understand that Bryce wasn't the most humble or kind guy. I also understand that he was wanted for the murder of four other young women who lived in that motel." Dr. Katz adjusted his posture in his chair and set his clipboard on the table beside him. "How did you know about all this? Was he a lover—or did you stumble across some information on him? Did you follow him with the purpose of killing him?"

Elaine hated to be pushed, and she felt trapped. She wanted this to stop quickly. "Doctor, I didn't know him any longer than that night. He tried to pick me up in the bar at the motel. I turned him down and went to the bathroom. When I came out, he was gone. That's it!"

"May I show you something?" Dr. Katz leaned forward on his desk.

Elaine shrugged. She knew she didn't have much choice in the matter. She knew he was trying to help her, but he didn't know what he was asking of her—and she was going to do everything possible to keep her secret.

"I want you to look through these and tell me what you see," he said.

Elaine reached across the desk and picked up the manila envelope. She had an increasingly bad feeling about its contents. When she looked at the pile of photos, her stomach churned. Staring her in the face was Bryce's cold, dead gaze. She pushed the photos back into the envelope and chucked them back onto the desk. "Why the hell would you show me these?"

"Elaine, please understand that I am trying to help you. I saw something in the photos that didn't quite make sense. I'm wondering if you would explain it for me. If you'd only just met the man, why would you write that he was bad and had to die?"

The bubble of safety she had built up over the past year was about to burst.

"I'm telling you the truth. What difference does it make what was written on the wall? It was still me who was found guilty of the murder and sent here—and that's all there is to it! Maybe this is where I should be."

Dr. Katz was fearful of pushing her too far, but he wanted her to come to grips with her actions and get better. He thought she had a chance, and he knew that showing her the photos was a risk. He felt that it would be the only thing that would make her open up to him about that night.

He'd known that she never had a straight story when she was arrested. At her trial, she did nothing to defend herself or protest. Her own mother didn't even take the stand for her. She just sat there and looked ahead.

Dr. Katz knew Elaine was developing relationships with her roommate and others. She was capable of allowing people into her protective walls. He could not believe that she—someone with as big a chance as any—would want to just stay there and exist. For the first time, he was at a loss. He barely had a scrap of information about her in comparison to the open-and-shut cases he'd come to know.

Elaine was not feeling well; her head was reeling and pounding. She'd not felt a migraine like that in a year, and her legs felt too weak to hold her. "Dr. Katz, can we please stop for now? I don't feel well." She clutched the wooden arm of the chair like it was her only connection to the world. A piercing pain passed through her skull. She crushed the arm of her chair and fell to the floor.

Dr. Katz rushed to her side and shouted for Nurse Hadler to grab some orderlies and a stretcher. He knelt down and felt for a pulse. It was weak.

They put Elaine on the stretcher and hurried to an observation room.

When Elaine regained consciousness, she started to thrash about violently.

Sarah, who had been leaning out of the doorway of the television room, watched them as they rushed by. She stepped into the hallway. "Dr. Katz, where are you taking Elaine? We have the movie on."

He turned over his shoulder and let the others continue on without him.

"Sarah, I'm afraid Elaine needs to go with us for a little while. Everything's fine, really it is, and she'll see you in a bit. Now, please head back with the others."

She nodded and turned, moving briskly back to her friends to tell them what happened.

When he caught back up to Nurse Hadler and the orderlies, Elaine was conscious on the bed. "Dr. Katz, what happened?"

"It appears that you had a seizure." He moved to her bedside.

"A seizure? But I don't have any seizure disorders."

"You've never had one before?" He was using his penlight to check her eyes as they spoke.

"No, I used to get really bad headaches, but I haven't had one of those the whole time I've been here—until just now."

He tucked his penlight into his coat pocket. "We're going to have to run some tests. In the meantime, I'm going to give you something for that headache. Just try to get some rest."

Elaine felt strange as they wrapped padding around the bed rails and secured it with tape. She didn't expect her head to be capable of hurting even more, but the pain was starting to become unbearable.

Dr. Katz soon appeared with a syringe.

Elaine's pain was horrific; she needed the medicine, but she hated needles to the point of panic. She shot upright in bed, smacked the syringe out of his hand, and screamed, "No! Get away from me! You're trying to kill me. I won't let you! Get away, you bad, bad man!" Elaine flailed through the grips of the orderlies and attempted to bite at the doctor.

Dr. Katz picked up the syringe and got a sterile one. "Elaine, listen. You have to try to calm down. It's going to be all right. It's only something to help you sleep through the pain. It's very important that you cooperate."

She was crying as she tried to pry herself free. "No, Dr. Katz! Please don't do this to me. I'm begging you. I'll be all right. I promise. Please don't!"

He pricked her with the needle and said, "I'm sorry, Elaine, but it has to be done until we figure out what's wrong with you."

She felt the rush of Thorazine and slipped into oblivion. Cinder had risen.

CHAPTER 2

Elaine slept soundly, restraints comfortably in place.

When Carrie Hadler's shift ended at midnight, she went to sit with Elaine. She had been working at Willow Tree for close to five years and had seen many patients go through quickly, but she knew Elaine was different. After an hour, she took another glance at the monitors and decided to call it a night. She collected her bag and walked out to the nurses' station.

Melissa Patterson was chatting with an orderly.

"Hey guys, I'm taking off for the night," Carrie said.

"Okay, Carrie. Drive safe," Melissa said.

Kyle nodded and returned his attention to Nurse Patterson.

Carrie had to wonder what Melissa could see in that orderly. She had heard enough about the way he made passing glances at the female patients. She could have sworn she heard the faintest voice behind her, whispering, "Creepy Kyle." She spun around with a small gasp, but no one else was in the hallway. Chuckling nervously to herself, she continued out of the building. *That's what happens when you stay later and don't go to bed early. Now we're hearing things.* When she reached her car, she dug through her purse for her keys. She sighed. *I could have sworn I put them in here, wait a second. I had them in my hand when I went into Elaine's room. They are on her nightstand. I swear I'd lose my own head. Gotta go all the way back now.*

Kyle was doing about everything he could to get Nurse Patterson to let him cop a feel. Melissa liked Kyle, but she knew that he was not the kind of guy for a solid relationship. Since everything was quiet, she figured it might be fun to pass the time with a man instead of a crossword puzzle and leftover Chinese. *Just as long as we don't get caught.* Maybe she'd allow a little heavy petting, but if he wanted to go any further, he was going to have to wait until they had the day off.

He was kissing her neck, making her giggle.

"Kyle, that tickles. Stop for a minute. I've gotta check on Elaine."

He breathed against her neck. "Oh, come on. Look at the monitors. She's fast asleep. It's fine."

She chuckled again and cupped his cheek. "All right, but just for a few more minutes—then I really do have to go check on her."

Just as Kyle was pulling the buttons of her blouse to claim his prize, the loud buzzing of the alarms came through the monitor, knocking Kyle off his chair.

Melissa jumped back, successfully dispensing him onto his face on the floor. She rushed into Elaine's room. She was having another seizure. "Oh, Jesus. Her straps are off. Kyle!"

Kyle moved to Elaine's other side and started to hold her down. "How the hell did her straps get off?"

"She's going to pull out her IV if we don't get them back on."

They were both struggling with her thrashing.

"We need help." Melissa ran out of the room to get Dr. Katz, leaving Kyle alone with Elaine.

Her eyes were rolling back, and Kyle's patience was wearing thin. "Sit still, you crazy bitch." He slapped her face, knocking her to the floor. "Shit." He grabbed her and tried to get her back into the bed. He'd be fired for sure if anyone saw that. He'd have to go back and remove a tape or two. It wouldn't be the first weird thing to happen around this girl. An unseen force threw him onto the bed, knocking the wind out of him.

He tried to get up, but he was strapped to the bed. He felt a weight on his chest, and fear prevented him from screaming. The more he struggled, the tighter the restraints became. His stomach was reeling, and he shut his eyes tightly. He was eager to open them again and find himself in his bed after this horrible bad dream, but when he opened his eyes, a creature was sitting on his chest. It had long, stringy black hair and the biggest, blackest eyes he had ever seen. It opened its mouth and revealed a set of jagged, mangled teeth. He thought the tongueless, bleeding creature might swallow him whole. Instead of being consumed, he heard women chanting to him over and over in a singsong pattern. They chanted, "Creepy Kyle, Creepy Kyle." The chants began to meld with the horrified sound of screaming and pleading. He came to the realization that the voices were from the women he had "played" with over the years.

An unbearable stinging pain tore at his abdomen and spread through his body. He tried to struggle out of the restraints, but the creature's demented maw curved up into a jagged smile. It drew closer to his chest, and Kyle watched in terror as it drew up its long, bony fingers and traced them over the pounding pulse in his neck. With a single flick of its wrist, he was reduced to a thrashing mess. Blood poured from his throat as its claws carved across his neck, gashing out his arteries and windpipe.

A bubbling froth of spit and blood spilled down his chin. A stream of blood trickled down to the floor. The creature showed itself no longer; Kyle's corpse was alone once more with Elaine.

Carrie stood in the doorway, witnessing the aftermath. Kyle's body jerked violently, convulsing and oozing blood.

Dr. Katz ran to the side of the bed and looked down at Kyle. "What on God's green earth happened in here? Nurse Patterson, I demand an answer! What happened here?"

Melissa nearly jumped out of her skin and looked at him with her eyes wide in disbelief. "Dr. Katz, please believe me when I say I have absolutely no idea! I left Kyle here to get Elaine back into her restraints. I rushed over to find you!"

Carrie knelt at Elaine's side, frantically feeling for a pulse. She sighed in relief at the faintest rhythmic thumping against her middle and index finger.

Dr. Katz affirmed Elaine's condition.

Melissa braced her back against the doorframe, trembling violently as tears pressed at her eyes.

Carrie quickly got to her feet, threw her arm around Melissa, and turned her gaze away.

"I swear it," Melissa said. "I swear I don't know how he got there. I went to get help. I was gone no more than five minutes!"

Carrie rubbed her back soothingly.

"Who would do such a sick thing, Carrie?" Melissa choked out another round of sobs.

Carrie lowered her chin onto Melissa's head and shut her eyes. She did not have an answer for her, and she was just as shocked as the others.

Dr. Katz made his way out of the room and returned with a pair of orderlies and a stretcher. They lifted Elaine off the floor and carted her to another room.

Dr. Katz called his wife and told her not to wait up for him. He gave Melissa a medicinal aid, and she was resting comfortably on the couch in his office.

A few minutes later, Willow Tree was teeming with police.

CHAPTER 3

Within the hour, Willow Tree was crawling with police. CSI agents dusted away and scoured the crime scene.

Elaine had yet to wake from her second seizure and was settled into her new room.

Carrie was rubbing her temples at the nurses' station in a fruitless attempt to rid herself of an oncoming headache. She was finding it more and more difficult to wrap her head around any of the questions she was asking herself. *Who put Kyle in the restraints if Elaine was seizing on the floor?* The police made the hall feel claustrophobic.

Dr. Katz and an inspector were talking in the hallway. The man lifted his eyes to meet Carrie's stare, and Dr. Katz looked over his shoulder before nodding. The men exchanged a few more words before the man walked over to Carrie. She took in a slow breath to steady her thoughts.

He spoke without the slightest trace of a smile. "Miss Hadler, I am Detective Eubanks. If you don't mind, I was hoping you'd be able to answer a few questions for me." She guessed he was in his forties. He had deep brown eyes and thick black hair. He reminded her of one of those hard-ass, no-nonsense cops on TV, but she could sense softness buried somewhere underneath all of that.

"Of course, whatever I can help with." She shifted in her seat.

"It's true that your shift ended at five?"

"Yes, but I decided to stay a little while longer out of my concern for Elaine."

He shifted his weight onto one foot. "You always stay late with your patients?"

"No, but Elaine is one of the patients I am closest to. That's all."

"Did you see what happened tonight?"

"No, I actually left the room about ten minutes before, but I ended up having to come back. I left my car keys on the nightstand. I got to the room while Dr. Katz and Nurse Patterson were rushing down the hall."

"And what did you see when you entered the room?"

Carrie swallowed. She was in no way a squeamish woman, but what she'd witnessed had disturbed her. She felt a lump in her throat. "Well, I saw Kyle strapped down to the bed, and Elaine was on the floor."

"What condition was she in when you left her to go to your car?"

"She was sleeping, stable."

"And where were Kyle and Ms. Patterson?"

"They were at the observation desk right here. He isn't usually around, and I figured they were visiting each other. It sounded like small talk when I was leaving."

"Did you see anyone else?"

"No, it's usually very quiet at night. We only keep a staff of about six here this late." She furrowed her brow.

Detective Eubanks parted his lips to continue his thorough investigation, but an officer flagged him down. The detective excused himself before leaving.

Carrie watched the two talk for a moment before he returned.

"Miss Hadler, does the phrase 'Creepy Kyle' mean anything to you?"

She felt like she could faint, and she was thankfully levelheaded enough to maintain her composure. A war was raging in her head. *Who could even know about what she called him if she'd never said it out loud?* "No, sir. I can't say that it does. Why do you ask?"

"Because it seems whoever was in the room with him made their escape through the stairwell and left a message there: Creepy Kyle hurts Phoebe, had to die. Apparently it was written in his own blood."

She knew she'd gotten there right after the fact since blood was still pouring from his body. *How could someone slip away that quickly?* She was sure no one was hiding and waiting for them to leave the room.

"Do you suppose Phoebe could have been somewhere—"

"No. Absolutely not, Detective. That's not possible. Phoebe is here because she was hurt—not for hurting anyone."

Detective Eubanks heaved a low sigh before resting his hands on his belt.

"Well, you see … that poses a big problem here. Because if she didn't do it, and nobody here did it, then it would've had to have been Elaine. She must have been tossed down in a struggle, went into some sort of fit, strapped him down, killed him, and then collapsed after the fact."

"Detective, that's way off. Elaine just had a seizure and was too weak and heavily sedated." It came out a little harsher than she would care to admit, her protective instincts getting the better of her.

"It's possible that the seizure could have been faked—and she seized the opportunity to strike when Nurse Patterson left the room."

Carrie was just about fed up with this asshole. He was grasping at straws. He knew nothing about Elaine or Phoebe—and who was he to make these kinds of assumptions anyway? "Or it's possible that Elaine and Phoebe were working together—"

"Detective, if you don't mind, perhaps we can continue this at a later time when I've had some time to sleep. It's been a long night for everyone, and I'd really like to be in bed after a glass of scotch."

"Are you a big drinker, Miss Hadler? Or do you only do it when you're trying to hide something?"

She flashed him a rather nasty look before walking away from him. She found Dr. Katz in his office. "Hey, how're you feeling?" she asked.

"A little groggy, but otherwise all right—if you can call it that. That look on his face … it was horrific. I'm afraid that whoever did this might still be here. Who will they come after next?"

Dr. Katz and Carrie sat down beside Melissa on the couch.

"Melissa, it's going to be all right," Carrie said. "I promise you."

"This was all my fault. If I hadn't left him, he would never have ended up like this!"

Dr. Katz put a hand on her shoulder. "Don't you think for one moment that anything was your fault."

"He's right," Carrie said. "Getting help was the right thing to do. You aren't to blame."

Carrie crossed to room to grab Melissa a few tissues, turning back around to see her favorite person of the evening as he approached the couch.

"Hello, Miss Patterson. I'm Detective Eubanks. Do you think you'd be up to answering a few questions for me?"

Dr. Katz said, "Detective, perhaps this conversation could wait until morning when she's had a chance to come down from shock."

Detective Eubanks nodded curtly. "If you'd like, you could come down to the station in a few hours. We can go over what happened then."

"No. I guess we can do it now and just get it out of the way." She took a tissue from Carrie and cleared her nose.

"Why was Kyle at the nurses' station with you?"

She dried her eyes on a second tissue. "He was on his break and came over to keep me company while I watched Elaine."

"Were the two of you good friends?"

Melissa flushed with embarrassment, not wanting anyone to think she was the kind of girl to fool around when working. She knew that was what Kyle was attempting to do, and she hadn't exactly told him no. Dr. Katz would be incredibly upset if he knew she diverted her attention from Elaine for that purpose. "We weren't that close. We'd only started talking a few days prior."

"What did you do when Elaine's monitors went off?"

"I jumped up and ran into her room."

"And where was Kyle?"

"He came in right behind me. We found Elaine seizing on the floor and out of her restraints. We were trying to get her back into bed before she ripped her IV out. It was hard for us. I left Kyle alone with her and went to go get help. When I came back … Kyle was … well … I'm sorry, Detective. I don't think I can do this … not now."

Carrie placed a hand on Melissa's shoulder. "Detective, can't you see she's had enough right now?"

Dr. Katz said, "I agree. Perhaps you should hold off on any more questions."

Detective Eubanks said, "I supposed that's all for now. I'll be in touch." He handed Melissa his card and walked out.

All three of them were more than ready to head home. They left the hospital together and went their separate ways in the parking lot.

CHAPTER 4

By the time the police had cleared the facility, the graveyard staff had begun additional bed checks. The patients were able to sleep once they were assured of their safety.

Sarah slept soundly, curled up on her side with Tobbie snuggled in her arms. She'd been the hardest one to console. Elaine was very important to her, and she was not able to join her in their room for the rest of the night. Sarah finally gave in to sleep after a much encouragement and a mild sedative.

Down the hall, Phoebe was also sleeping peacefully. Joan was allowed to join her and sleep in the spare bed. Joan always had a soft spot for Phoebe, thinking of her as the child she always wanted but never got to have. Being bipolar made it nearly impossible to have children; the doctors found it to be too much of a risk to go off of her medications.

Miles was not as lucky as the rest of the patients. He was plagued by terrible nightmares about his his former fiancée. Gina chased him through the home they shared before her demise at his hands. He would struggle to get free of her, but she would always find his hiding places. She was bloodied, and the gaping bullet wound in her chest was big enough to see through. He tried not to look at her if he could help it, but she laughed eerily and said, "Miles, come out, come out, where ever you are."

He could smell her; she stunk heavily of rotting. She was getting closer and closer the more he ran. She had once been such a beautiful visage, but she had twisted into some grotesque entity. He was sure she was trying to kill him. He was nearly trapped in her grasp before the bright glare of a penlight flashed in his eyes.

"Miles?" Nurse Paula leaned back and looked down at him. "You all right, buddy?"

He squinted as she moved the light out of his face. He nodded and rubbed his face. "I guess … I'm sorry. I was having a bad dream. I wasn't screaming, was I?"

She shook her head and smiled lightly. "No. You were just thrashing around, but I can't blame you. It's been a rough night for everyone. Want some water?" She stood up.

"Yeah, that'd be great. Thanks."

She poured him a glass and handed it over.

He sat up, drank it slowly, and set the glass aside.

"You get some rest now, Miles. I will be back to check on you in just a few."

He nodded and let his head fall back on the pillow. When she left the room, he thought back to his nightmare. He dreamed of Gina often, but it was never anything like that. They had always been so soothing. He'd never associated her with anything remotely scary. He would have to talk to Dr. Katz about it at his next session.

The following morning, Willow Tree looked just as normal as ever. The grounds remained the same, and the sun was still rising in the east to wake the birds so they could start their songs. Inside, however, was a different atmosphere altogether.

Dr. Katz had a sleepless night at home and decided to come back to work early.

Detective Eubanks was waiting for him in the TV room. Dr. Katz was not eager to speak with the detective again so soon, but he grabbed a cup of coffee and headed to meet him.

Detective Eubanks stood when the doctor walked in. "Dr. Katz, thank you for seeing me again."

"Detective Eubanks, I believe I have told you everything I know. I already gave you a signed statement about what I saw. I am baffled about why you happen to be here now."

"Dr. Katz, I've been thinking a lot about what happened after Miss Patterson left. Miss Cooper and Kyle were supposedly the only ones in the room. Do you suppose it was possible that she could have faked a seizure and attacked him?"

"Detective, she was under heavy sedation in the hopes of preventing a second seizure—and she was restrained to the bed."

"Yes, though it says in Miss Patterson's statement that her restraints were off when she returned to the room. Did you have them removed for any reason? Do you think anyone here would have removed them?"

"No. I cannot for the life of me think of anyone who would do that. No one on my staff would do anything without specific instructions from me. Detective, Elaine had no motive to kill Kyle. He was an orderly she barely knew."

"Was there a reason she killed the other guy then?"

"I'm not discussing that with you. There is a thing called doctor-patient confidentiality. I want to find the culprit too, but look someplace else. It's not Elaine."

Joan pushed through the doorway. She was frantic and out of breath. "Doctor, thank God I found you." She crossed the room to him "You've gotta come quick. It's Phoebe!"

"What? What's wrong with Phoebe?"

"Just hurry! Come see!" Joan ran back into the hallway with the doctor and the detective in tow. When they made it to Phoebe's room, they were stunned.

Phoebe was pacing back and forth, clutching a fat black marker in her hand. She had written at least twenty times on all four walls: *Kyle and Bryce were bad bad had to Die. They Had to Die.* The messages overlapped in places where she'd run out of room. She was spitting, grunting, and pulling at her hair with her free hand. Her breathing was ragged and uneven. She let out a scream and collapsed.

"Phoebe!" Dr. Katz rushed to her side.

"Dear God, Phoebe," Joan said.

"Joan, quick. Go get help."

She nodded and spun around, almost knocking the stunned detective off his feet. "Move, you ass!" she shouted as she shoved him out of her way.

Dr. Katz cradled Phoebe's head in his lap while he took in the room's condition

"Dr. Katz, was this woman involved in what happened last night?" the detective asked.

"For Christ's sake, Detective, can this wait? Can't you see she's in distress? Phoebe had nothing to do with any of that. She's a passive case! She's never acted like this before."

Joan ran back inside with two orderlies and Carrie at her heels. "Jesus Christ! Did Phoebe do all of this? Carrie, she's burning up. We need to get her into bed and get her temperature down."

They shoved Detective Eubanks over to the corner of the doorway and helped Phoebe into the bed.

Phoebe was mumbling incoherently, and her fever spiked dangerously high. They covered her body in cold packs and sent for an IV drip. They feared for the condition of her brain as she peaked at 106 degrees.

The detective stayed out of the way as they all worked to bring her temperature down.

Joan held her hand and whispered to her.

It took an hour to break her fever, and they all kept her under close watch.

Phoebe's eyes fluttered. She blinked a few times, slowly, before turning her head to look over at Joan. "Hello, sweetheart."

Joan smiled. "It's good to see your pretty eyes again."

Phoebe looked over at the detective.

Carrie lifted her head and followed her gaze before smiling. "That's Detective Eubanks, Phoebe. Don't worry. He's not going to hurt you. She's not too fond of strangers." She lifted her hand and pointed at him.

"You want me to come over there?" Eubanks asked, moving slowly to her side, watching her lower her hand and smile gently to him.

Carrie looked to the others and found them just as surprised as she was that she wanted a stranger to be this this close to her.

Phoebe was whispering inaudibly.

"I can't understand you." Detective Eubanks put his arm over the bed to keep himself from falling on top of her. He leaned in close to her face.

She slowly brought her lips to his ear and shouted, "Fucker!" Her hands clamped down on his arm, and she dug her teeth into it, causing him to yell and yank on his appendage, Phoebe's grip held as she broke his skin and ripped at it with a grunt.

The doctor quickly got some Thorazine and put it through her drip before everyone was around Phoebe. Carrie tried to hold her head to keep her from twisting it and yanking his arm.

"Would you hurry up?" Eubanks shouted.

"Give her a minute!" Dr. Katz said. "Just stay still and calm. When the sedative kicks in, she'll let you go.

After half a minute, she released her death grip.

The detective jerked his arm away to evaluate the damage.

Carrie quickly wrapped his arm to help control the bleeding. "You're going to need stitches on that bite. When's the last time you had a tetanus shot?" she asked, taking in a long, deep breath.

"Not one that I can remember," he replied.

"Well, you're gettin' one today. Human bites can be just as bad as animal ones—if not worse."

"She damn near took my whole arm off. Passive my ass," he growled to himself.

"What she did is nowhere near anything like how she normally behaves. She's never attacked anyone. It may have been her fever."

"Or maybe she had something to do with last night. Phoebe and Elaine were probably working together," he stated flatly, wincing at his arm.

"Detective, if you knew these girls anywhere near as well as we all do, you would be saying no such thing about either of them. What you're accusing them of is absurd." She joined the doctor as he wiped the last of the detective's blood off of Phoebe's face.

A nurse came rushing in. She was out of breath and holding her side. "Dr. Katz, I apologize for interrupting, but it's Elaine. She's convulsing again with a dangerously high fever, and we can't get it to stop."

He followed after the nurse. "What in the hell is going on today?" He rushed out of the room and left the three alone with Phoebe.

"Detective," Carrie started, "why don't you go down to the nurse's station and tell Mary that you need stitches and a tetanus shot. Joan, you should go meet Sarah. I've got to help the doctor." She exited the room quickly, Joan following behind her.

Detective Eubanks called the station and requested the files on Elaine and Phoebe, barking about wanting the CSI back at the scene before snapping his phone shut. He went off to find Mary and get patched up while he waited for the police to show.

CHAPTER 5

Dr. Katz and his team were having a hell of a time trying to get Elaine's convulsions to stop. The Atavan had absolutely no effect until the third dose. When she had finally calmed down, Carrie sat down in the chair next to her bed while Dr. Katz wrote out the new orders for Elaine. He knew her body would not be able to handle any more of these seizures; there would be brain damage if they kept up. Her fever was also a great concern. Here were two relatively healthy women who had bizarre episodes and high fevers in the same day for no apparent reason. At first, he thought they had both come into contact with something, but the blood test results proved him wrong. There was no trace of anything that would bring on these behaviors. Whatever was going on with them, it wasn't medical.

Carrie sat with her head tilted back and her eyes closed. She just wanted everything to go back to the days where it was boring and normal. As more things happened, she felt that normal might never be achieved again—at least the sense of normal she'd come to know so familiarly.

Detective Eubanks had finished up with his stitches, and the hospital was crawling with police officers. CSI were photographing every inch of Phoebe's room and the names scrawled over the walls.

Once she was stable, Phoebe was secured and placed in a protective room. Detective Eubanks watched as they carted her down the hall in four-point restraints, her eyes trained up at the ceiling in an almost catatonic trance.

He was having a hard time believe that she was harmless. He had a total of eighteen stitches to back up his opinion of her. If she were given the chance, she would have happily taken his entire arm clean off. He was staring at the names on the walls and wondering what the hell all of it could mean. He was deep in though when a uniformed officer he didn't recognized approached him.

"Detective Eubanks?" A middle-aged officer was standing in the doorway with a manila file in her hand.

"Yes, may I help you?" He raised a brow and looked at the file.

"I'm Patricia Torres. I heard that you were interested in obtaining the police files for … Elaine Cooper?"

"No offense, ma'am, but what exactly does that information have to do with you?"

Officer Torres smiled and shifted her weight onto her right foot. "None taken—just figured I'd bring it to you myself."

He raised a brow further and put a hand on his hip. "The station could have just faxed everything over to me. What's the fuss all about?"

She took a step into the room. "Well, I was first reporting at the hotel where Bryce Freeman's body was found in her room."

He shifted his weight. "So you've met Miss Cooper then?"

"Yes, sir. She was a real mess. She had to be carted off in an ambulance—and that hotel room? Phew, it was something out of one of those gory flicks. Blood was everywhere. Photos are in the folder, and I hope you've got a strong stomach." She held it out to him.

He took the file and flipped it open. The photos were all in the front. Elaine had really done a number on the guy. The room looked like she'd been trying to paint it.

"Detective Eubanks, I have been at this job for many, many years—and let's just say that a weapon capable of that kind of damage to his throat would not be easy to hide. With the state she was in when we found her, I don't believe she was coherent enough to hide herself—let alone a large weapon. I hope that's been a little helpful, but I've gotta be heading back now."

"Wait. Just a few more questions please. Does Elaine have any family in the area that you know of?"

She turned back to face him. "Her mother lives in Jersey, and her father died a few years back in some kind of freak accident. The poor bastard lost his footing on the roof and impaled himself on a metal fencepost. By the time his wife got back, it was already far too late for him."

His brow furrowed. "Was Elaine there at the time?"

"Yes, I believe she'd arrived the day before."

"Have you met Elaine's mother?"

She nodded and put her hand on her hip. "Yeah, I had to testify at her trial, and she was there. She's a real piece of work. She said Elaine was nothing but trouble, always an ungrateful child, and more along the same lines. She didn't have a whole lot of good to say about her daughter, and I didn't see any love between them."

"Thank you for your time, Officer Torres. I really appreciate the information."

They exchanged cards and departed with a handshake. She couldn't get out of that place fast enough, it seemed, making a swift exit after a curt good-bye.

Eubanks was left with a lot of information to process. He had originally wanted to investigate Phoebe further, but with this new information, he doubted it would be necessary. He had a feeling that whatever was going on was centered on Elaine. She was definitely a woman with an abundance of secrets—secrets that he was determined to dig up and link her to everything about this mess. All the nurses who wanted to try to cover for her and protect her were going down with her—every last one.

CHAPTER 6

Over the next twenty-four hours at Willow Tree, Nurse Patterson resigned from her job, Phoebe was placed in a padded isolation room, regressing to the behaviors she exhibited when she arrived at the facility, and Joan was praying for everyone. Sarah was still rather pissed about Elaine, deciding to spend most of her time with Miles. Unfortunately, he was not doing very well.

That afternoon, he had his session with Dr. Katz.

"Miles, I know that things have been particularly traumatic around here as of late, to say the least, but I would like to know how you're holding up?"

Miles sighed. "I've been having nightmares about the night I killed Gina. I've had dreams about us before, but they were never like this. She's bloody now, and she's always calling out to me."

"And how does this make you feel, Miles."

"To be completely honest, it scares the shit out of me. I'm afraid of going to sleep."

Dr. Katz nodded and jotted something in his notebook. "These dreams you're having could have been brought on by Kyle's tragic death. I'll modify your medications and up your dose so you can sleep more soundly. I want you to write in your journal. We can discuss the contents at our next session. Sound like a plan to you?"

Miles nodded. "I just want the nightmares to stop."

After dinner, Sarah and Joan watched a movie together. Miles said he wasn't up to it and went to his room to try to get a decent night's sleep. Dr. Katz had approved his request to have his medication early.

Sarah and Joan decided to go with *As Good as It Gets*. Joan secretly loved Jack Nicholson. She thought he was the sexiest man she'd ever laid eyes on. The two women ate popcorn, and Sarah laughed so hard at one point that Joan thought she might choke.

Joan enjoyed the movies. They reminded her of when she would host movie nights for her friends at her cute Spanish bungalow, a place she took a great deal of care in decorating.

Her teaching salary never brought in much as far as income went, but she took her time and collected everything. It was sad that everyone could not be there to join them for the movie. Joan could hear Phoebe screaming and crying when she was on the way to her session, and it broke Joan's heart to hear it.

Things were changing—and not for the better. Kyle had been killed, and all of Joan's friends were in trouble. She never really cared for Kyle. One night when she was not quite asleep, she caught the bastard sneaking into her room and trying to stuff his hands up her nightgown. He told her that Dr. Katz wouldn't believe a crazy old crone who stabbed her friend. She wasn't sure if she was angrier about him trying to feel her up or him trying to insinuate that she was old! He laughed at her and left her room with a whistled tune. *What a creep.*

Yes, he was quite the bad seed—and he got what he deserved. *Have a little of that, fuckhead,* she thought, smiling to herself. She looked over at Sarah and caught her yawning. The movie had ten minutes left, and it was just about time for medications and sleep.

When the movie ended, she and Sarah waited in line at the nurses' station and got their meds. They walked down the hall together and said their good-byes when they reached Sarah and Elaine's room.

"Hope you sleep well, Sarah."

"I hope I do too. It's tough being in my room without Elaine there. She used to have me count Tobbies when I couldn't sleep. Do you think she'll wake up soon?"

"Elaine just needs some time to rest up right now, Sarah. I am sure she'll come back to us when she's ready. Maybe we could ask Dr. Katz if we could come in and sit with her for a little while tomorrow. I hear that people who are comatose have a higher chance of waking up if they're stimulated by people's voices."

Sarah smiled and nodded. "Thanks, Joan. Sleep well. I hope Miles feels better soon too. Maybe he'll want to go with us to see Elaine. I really hope so."

Joan smiled. "Me too, kiddo. Good night."

Sarah closed the door and changed into her favorite pajamas: the pink, short-sleeved shirt with little black dogs on it and matching long bottoms. She'd always wanted a real dog, but her parents always told her they were much too much work and that no one had the time to train one properly. Rebecca had gotten Tobbie at Beeman's Department Store about a week before Sarah's birthday. He was so soft and yellow with his floppy ears. Sarah begged her mother for him, but it wasn't in the budget—whatever that meant. Sarah was heartbroken and carried it around with her till they were through with their shopping. At the checkout counter, the cashier asked if she wanted the dog rung up too. Her mother sharply replied, "No," and she shoved the dog onto the counter.

Rebecca had gone back later and spent all her babysitting money on him as her birthday present. She told Sarah that there was nothing more important than putting a smile on her baby sister's face. Sarah missed her sister very much at times. Sarah climbed into bed, squeezed Tobbie tightly to her chest, and snuggled up to him under the covers. It was not long before she was asleep.

CHAPTER 7

At one in the morning, the staff had just finished a round of bed checks. Dr. Katz had long since gone home, and Carrie had decided to take a few personal days, which he couldn't blame her for. There were a couple of night-shift orderlies playing cards to pass the time between checks. A few nurses were catching up on paperwork at the main nurses' station. One of them had popped in on Phoebe earlier and found her curled up in the corner on her mat with her thumb stuck in her mouth.

Miles was staring at the ceiling. The pills had put him to sleep, but they were not doing their job of keeping him that way. It was dark, and he tried to fix his concentration on good thoughts, like Sarah. She'd always try to make him feel better. She was so very kind and sweet. Every Sunday night, they'd have butterscotch pudding for dessert; she'd always share hers with him. Miles looked over when he heard the door creak open. A sick feeling pooled in the pit of his stomach. They'd just done a bed check; who was it?

Miles sat up, and the color drained from his body. A chilling fear glued him to his place, breaking into a cold sweat. Gina moved toward him from the doorway. Her flesh had decayed, and her gaping wound oozed with congealed and chunky blood. Her hollow eyes seemed to bore a hole in him. He tried to bring his knees up to his chest, but in his panic-stricken state, he was unable to move.

As Gina parted her lips and tilted her head, the sound of her crackling joints and bones echoed quietly through the room. "Miles," she called hauntingly, hands outstretched, fingers twisted, and contorted unnaturally as she moved

33

closer. "Miles, come to me, my love. Don't you want to? I need you. Don't you want to make love to me?" Gina crawled up from the foot of his bed, trapping his legs under her as he scooted as far against the wall as he could. It was no use trying to escape. She was nearly on top of him. Miles squeezed his eyes shut and sunk into his reassuring thoughts. *No no no. This is just another fucked-up dream. This isn't real. When I open my eyes, she'll be gone.* When he let his eyes fall on his room again, she had climbed onto his lap and was dominating his field of view.

"No, Miles. This isn't a dream, baby. I am very real." She reached down and grabbed his wrist, lifting his hand. "Here. Touch me." She pushed his palm against her breast, cooing.

Miles felt like he was going to be sick. She was not the soft Gina he knew, the one he wished to marry. She was rotted, revolting flesh. It took every ounce of courage he could muster, but as she closed the distance between them, he let out a scream at the top of his lungs. "Help me! Help! Somebody get her the hell off me! Get her off!"

The screams sent the orderlies flying down the hall like their asses were on fire. The nurses burst into the room. Miles was white as a sheet, alone in his bed and swatting frantically at the air in front of him,

An orderly rushed over and took a seat on the side of his bed, gently catching his hands and lowering them. "Hey, Miles? It's Jake. You're all right, buddy. It's all okay. It's just another nightmare, okay? We're here." He reached over and turned on the lamp.

Miles wanted to make damn sure it was really Jake sitting next to him and that Gina had disappeared. He blinked a few times and reached out to touch Jake's shoulder.

One of the nurses poured a glass of water and handed it to Miles. He had to stop himself from slugging it down too quickly. He took slow, deep swallows and set the glass down on the nightstand.

While one of the nurses called the doctor, the others went out into the hall to calm the other patients and get them settled back into their rooms.

Miles already felt better surrounded by more people and under the comfort of a light. Jake got him more water, and Dr. Katz approved an order for an injection of Valium. Jake sat with him for a few minutes while the medicine kicked in, leaving the light on when he left.

No one saw the pair of red footprints that trailed out after him because they disappeared after he returned to his game of cards.

The next morning, Dr. Katz sat at his desk. He had not been able to sleep much after the call about Miles. Miles had been asleep when Dr. Katz arrived, and he did not want to disturb him, ordering that he should be left be until he woke up on his own. With the night he'd had, he was sure he could use the rest. When he finally did wake up, Dr. Katz hoped they could take their session outside and get some fresh air.

He picked up his notes on Phoebe that needed to be typed and filed away. She was another patient who would be requiring some extra time. All that work and progress she had made with trust seemed like it was slipping away. It pained him greatly, but he wasn't about to let her go down the tubes like that.

He had just gotten up to pour himself a cup of coffee when a nurse informed him that the detective was on the line for him. He had a feeling he wasn't going to like it very much. "This is Dr. Katz. How can I help you, Detective?"

"Hello, Doctor. The reason for my call today is that I wanted to inform you that I am on my way to New Jersey to see Elaine's mother. I wanted to know if you've informed her that her daughter is in a coma yet?"

"No, Detective. I have no way of reaching her, and to my understanding, I don't even think she owns a phone. Besides, I don't think she would care to hear about how Elaine was doing—or anything else about Elaine."

"Should I mention it?" the detective asked.

"I see no harm in it. However, I will tell you that I had a chance to meet Mrs. Cooper shortly after Elaine's arrival, and she did not want to see her. She came out all this way to tell me she thought Elaine should receive our most severe treatments, demanding shock therapy, and no less. To my utter disbelief, she was nearly enraged at my denial of her requests, telling me coddling her was no good. It would be recommended—and I highly advise—taking caution when it comes to that woman, Detective."

"Thank you for the heads-up, Doc. I'll get back to you if I find out anything that might be useful to you."

Dr. Katz nursed his coffee for a few minutes, deep in thought. If there was one person he never cared to hear from again, it definitely had to be Mrs. Cooper. She needed to be institutionalized somewhere instead of living a lonely life, but that might be punishment enough.

Carrie had slept in, which she hadn't done in quite some time, and she was glad for the extra rest. She was sitting in her chaise lounge and catching up on a mind-numbing, trashy novel and drinking green tea. Her basset hound was content at her feet. It felt good to have some time alone. She had never been fond of Kyle, but seeing him that way was one of the worst things she'd ever seen. She was having a difficult time wrapping her head around everything that had happened.

She knew the detective thought she was hiding something. She was sure of it. She had no idea how to begin explaining what happened, and even if she tried to, he never would have believed her. He'd probably think she was mad too. She and the other person who had witnessed it had decided not to tell a soul—and who would believe them if they did?

Elaine was the key—everyone was certain of it—but the problem was finding out what she unlocked. What would they find? Carrie decided to call Dr. Katz to see how things were going. She hoped that nothing else had happened and dreaded that he would tell her more bad news.

"Hi, Dr. Katz, it's Carrie. I was just calling to see how things were going on your end."

"Hello, Carrie. Things are going about as well as can be expected. Miles had a rather harsh night terror it seems. Are you resting well enough like I told you to?"

She smiled. "Yes, I've had some bad dreams, but that's to be expected after everything that's gone on. I'm already feeling better this morning. Any changes with Phoebe and Elaine?"

"No, nothing. Do you need me to prescribe you something to help with your sleep?"

"No thanks. I will be all right."

"Well, please just get some rest—and let me know if you happen to change your mind about the medication, all right?"

"I will. I just wanted to check in with you. I'll see you in the morning. Bye."

"Bye, Carrie. See you tomorrow."

Carrie changed into sweatpants and a Penn State T-shirt, put Moe on his leash, and went to the dog park.

When Dr. Katz got off the phone, Joan and Sarah were standing at his doorway. "Hello, ladies. How are you both doing today?"

"We're doing well," Joan answered. "We're sorry to bother you, but we were wondering if it would be possible to sit in with Elaine. We promise we won't stay too long."

He smiled. "I think that would be all right. I know how close you all are. As long as you keep your visit short—and things go all right—you may visit her tomorrow as well."

Sarah smiled. "Thank you, Dr. Katz. We promise—we really do."

"You're very welcome. If you want, you two can head down there now. I will call the nurse and let her know it's all right for the two of you to be there." He picked up the phone as they left the room.

CHAPTER 8

When Miles walked into Dr. Katz's office, he looked and felt like hell. He had dark circles under his eyes. He hadn't showered, and he was still wearing the sweatpants and T-shirt he'd slept in. His face was drawn, and his hair was pointed in every direction.

"Please come in, Miles," Dr. Katz said.

Miles shuffled over to the couch, keeping his head down.

"How about we take our session outside today? It's beautiful out, and I bet the fresh air would do you good. What do you say?" He leaned forward in his chair.

"I guess that would be all right." Miles didn't really feel like talking, but he knew that it would only be worse to keep everything in his head.

When they got outside, they took a seat under one of the old oak trees. Miles liked that particular tree; it reminded him of having a picnic lunch with Gina. It had been the spot where they celebrated getting their first home.

Dr. Katz flipped open his notebook and said, "Miles, are you up to talking about your nightmares last night? You gave the staff quite the jolt."

"Well, even though I know you aren't going to believe me, I was not asleep last night when I saw Gina. I was asleep before that, but I got woken up. I was lying there awake when I heard my door open. I thought it was the staff doing a night check, but they'd just come in. That's why I woke up."

The doctor frowned. "Miles, is it possible that you fell back asleep and just thought you were awake? Was it one of those dreams within a dream?"

Miles's rubbed his eyes and took a deep breath. "No, Dr. Katz. You have to believe me. I know for a fact that I was awake. I was upset that I had not slept through the night!"

"All right, Miles. You say you were awake, so you were awake. Would you like to continue?"

"I was staring up at the ceiling and thinking when I heard the door start to open. I said the whole thing about the night checks. I started to feel a pit in my stomach, and then I saw her in the doorway. I could smell her too—something rotten. She started moving toward me, saying my name, reaching out to me. It paralyzed me with fear." Miles shut his eyes tightly and tried to calm his breathing.

Dr. Katz reached over and put his hand on Miles's arm. "Easy, Miles. Just try to stay calm. You're all right. Take your time. What happened next?"

"She got into my bed and grabbed my hand, forcing me to feel her. She was saying she loved me and she wanted to … well, you know, be together, but she said it more crudely than I had ever heard her talk. It stunned me. She was a kind and decent woman, but last night, she was vulgar and creepy. I know she was there. I just know it. I screamed and shut my eyes when she got close to my face." He choked back his tears, wringing the bottom of his shirt in his hands. He was thankful he had skipped breakfast; otherwise, the doctor would be wearing it.

"All right, Miles." The doctor closed his notebook. "Why don't we take a break for now, okay? I want you to know that you aren't alone. We will get through this. I will do whatever it takes to get you back on track. There are ways to work through these kinds of things. I really need you to continue to write in your journal. I will switch out your medications. Kyle's death has taken a toll on a large group here, but it's possible that it's also affecting you."

Miles wanted desperately to believe that Kyle's death was bringing on the vivid nightmares, but he knew she was there—and nobody was going to tell him any different. He felt completely alone and scared of a woman he had once loved beyond words.

The doctor returned to his office, and Miles went to the TV room. He pulled a picture of Gina from his waistband. She was sitting beneath the old tree, holding a glass of blackberry merlot, her favorite, and smiling to herself. It was taken at their housewarming party, and everyone talked about their large wedding, which was being planned. Her parents were delighted to pay for the entire event—back when they were both happy.

CHAPTER 9

Joan and Sarah sat with Elaine for a solid hour. Sarah had chatted on and on, telling Elaine how much she missed her and wanted more than anything for her to wake up and talk to them. She also talked with her about how sad Phoebe was and how differently Miles was acting toward everyone. Joan prayed for most of the time and rubbed Elaine's arms and legs. She had heard that it was a good thing to do to people who were in a coma since it promoted circulation.

When they got ready to leave, Joan placed a kiss on Elaine's forehead and whispered, "When you're ready to wake up, we'll all be here waiting to see your beautiful eyes, sweet girl."

When Joan headed to her session, Sarah went into the TV room. She noticed the picture in Miles's hand and leaned in. "Hey Miles, who's that girl?"

Miles pulled the picture away.

She shrank back and twiddled her thumbs. "I'm sorry. I didn't mean to touch it. I wasn't gonna hurt it. I promise. She's pretty. Is she your friend?"

Miles sighed, reached up, and touched her hair. "She was my fiancée."

"Judy, right?"

"No, it was Gina."

"Sorry. I'm super bad with names. Can I see her? I promise I'll be super careful."

He slowly passed the picture to her.

"She is pretty. And she's drinking wine, right? I like her sweater. What's wine taste like, Miles?"

"It's like grape juice, but a little bitter." He smiled at her innocence of the world.

"Did you drink a lot of wine, Miles?"

"No. I was more of a beer drinker myself. Gina was the one who was really into wine."

She turned and kept her eyes down on the picture, her body facing him. "Please tell me more about her!"

His heart ached, and he really didn't want to talk about her, but it was impossible to say no to that face. Maybe it would help, and she was such a good listener. "What do you want to know?"

"What'd she smell like?" She held the picture closer to her face, examining every centimeter of it.

"She smelled like lavender because of the hand cream she always used."

"I like lavender. It smells good. What was she like, Miles?"

"Gina was a really sweet person—one of the sweetest to walk the earth. She never had a bad thing to say about anybody. She loved helping people, and she was putting herself through school to be a social worker. She wanted to adopt children, thinking there were already so many in the world who needed love and good homes. She wanted at least four."

Sarah admired Miles as he continued talking. She thought his glasses made him look really smart—and the look on his face made her wish he would talk about *her* in that way. She pointed down at the necklace in the photo. "I love the butterfly. I really like green. It's beautiful."

"Gina loved butterflies. I bought it for her on her last birthday before she … well, before she died."

"Butterflies are beautiful, and they're so lucky because they're free to go wherever they please. The colors on them are almost magical." Sarah carefully handed the picture back to him.

"Do you know what you want to wish for when you blow out the candles?"

She tapped her lower lip and squinted. "I know that I'm not supposed to say my wish out loud because it's bad luck, but you guys can keep a secret." She smiled. "I wish that somebody, someday, would love me enough to give me one of those beautiful necklaces. Does that sound stupid?"

He set her heart racing when he placed his hand on her wrist. "It isn't stupid at all, and I hope your birthday is as perfect as you want it to be. I really hope you like the gift I made for you."

Her face lit up. "You made me a present, Miles? Can I have a small hint?"

He folded his arms, smiled, and shook his head. "Nope—not even one teeny tiny hint." He placed his hand on the top of her head, giving her hair a gentle ruffle and making her blush.

"Oh, all right. If you say so."

One of the nurses came in to collect her for her session with Dr. Katz.

Sarah gave him a playful wink before bouncing out of the room behind the nurse.

CHAPTER 10

Sarah could barely sit still during her session. Nobody ever made her feel like that, and it made her rather happy that Miles did.

"How is your day going?" Dr. Katz asked.

Sarah smiled brightly. "Today is a really, really good day. I got to see Elaine, and Miles seemed a little happier, which is good. We got to talk for a little bit, and he says he made me something for my birthday." Her smile curved into a pout. "But he won't give me any hints. I'm a little disappointed that Phoebe and Elaine won't be there. I wish everything were the way it was before Kyle died."

"How do you feel about what happened to Kyle?"

"I dunno. I don't really feel anything about it. I know it's not really nice to say, but I really didn't like him."

Dr. Katz sat up in his chair. "Well, why's that?"

Sarah shrugged lazily. "He was just weird, and he stands too close to us girls—and the way he looked at Elaine when she didn't know? Yuck." She stuck out her tongue. "This one day, he was touching Phoebe all over the place. I yelled at him and told him to leave her alone 'cuz she didn't like it. He told me to shut my crazy ass up before he made sure I never spoke again. He was super mean."

"Sarah, why didn't you tell me about any of this?"

She looked down at her lap and folded her hands. "He said nobody would believe a crazy girl who killed her family."

"Sarah, always believe me when I say that you can come to me about anything. I promise that I'll believe you because I know you would never lie to me. Was there anything else he did?"

"No, it was that one time. I made super sure to make sure I kept Phoebe away from him while he was working. I don't wanna talk about him anymore. Let's stop."

"Sure. How about you go join Joan. I happen to know she's working on your birthday banner in the arts and crafts room. Would you like to go over and give her a hand?"

"I would like to—very much. Yes." Sarah got up and trotted down the hallway to see Joan.

That evening, Sarah, Joan, and Miles played Go Fish. The two women had worked on the birthday banner until dinner, and Joan had painted little dogs all over it that looked like Tobbie.

Miles sat across from Sarah. He liked watching her play cards. She always made the cutest faces, scrunching up her face when she was deciding what card to ask him or Joan for next and swinging her feet. He wished things could be different—that he and Sarah weren't confined to the hospital. He wanted to show her all his favorite places, and he knew she would love to go to a concert in the park and listen to music as they sipped wine. He could imagine her sitting on a big blanket in the grass, laughing and smiling.

Sarah had missed out on so much of what there was out there—the things that other people take for granted—and Miles wanted so badly to go out and buy her a big, beautiful present for her birthday. Since it was impossible, he put his heart into trying to make something as perfect as he could get it. Miles loved that she didn't mind in the least what he'd done and simply wanted to be around him. In return, he did not judge her for what she did when she was just a child. Maybe this was what they called *unconditional* love.

Sarah's giggles snapped him out of his thoughts. "Miles, are you going to go? We don't have all night, silly."

"Sorry, Sarah."

Joan could see that the two of them really cared about one another. *Who knew you could find love in a mental hospital?* She guessed anything was possible, and she knew stranger things could happen. She found it just the tiniest bit sad that they couldn't have a regular life together like other people in the world at their ages. They took what they could get, and it made them happy. She tried her best not to think too hard about it. They had found a little piece of paradise in their blank space, and she thought that was something special.

CHAPTER 11

Sarah could hardly contain herself as she leaped out of her bed and ran over to her closet. Her birthday was finally here, and she fished out the long-sleeved green dress with the big sunflowers on it that she'd gotten from the staff for Christmas the previous year.

Nurse Gabrielle was on shower duty that morning and smiled at Sarah. "Happy birthday to you, honey. Are you excited?"

"Yes, yes. I am so excited. Miles told me he made me something, and I know it's just going to be the most perfect and most beautiful present ever." Sarah hummed a light tune to herself as she showered and took great care to brush every single tangle out of her long red hair.

Sarah got dressed, and Gabrielle produced a little box from her pocket, holding it out to her. "Here, sweetie. You can have my present early."

Sarah beamed and took the box from as if it were the finest of gold. She carefully opened it and found two plastic combs with sunflowers on them. "Oh, Gabrielle. Thank you. They match my dress. They're perfect."

Gabrielle pulled back Sarah's hair and helped her to put them in, exposing her freckled cheeks and little ears. She felt like a princess.

When Sarah arrived at the breakfast table, Joan and Miles were waiting for her. Miles did a double take, finding her stunning with her hair out of her face.

Joan slid around to the other side of the table so that Sarah could take her seat next to Miles. "Wow, you look so very pretty, doesn't she Miles?" she said with a warm smile.

46

He swallowed and nodded with a smile. "Yeah, your hair looks very nice when it's pulled back a little like that."

Sarah was much too excited to eat. She took a few bites but mostly pushed the food around her plate and bounced in her seat.

Miles desperately wanted to tell her how he felt about her, but he felt that it wouldn't be fair to either of them. He knew their relationship could never be a normal one. He hated to admit it, but he knew he loved her more than he should. This love also made him feel guilty because he had loved Gina. She had been very special and dear to him, but look at what he'd done. He'd hurt something so precious. He would never forgive himself if he did anything to Sarah.

Dr. Katz had gone to work a little earlier than usual to spend some extra time working with Phoebe. He was putting in a little extra time with her each and every day, waiting until the end of the day to see her so he could spend more time working with her. She had started to show progress again, and he'd finally gotten her to stop sucking on her thumb. She had a long way to go, but he was pleased with each small victory. Today he was going to test her again. He wanted to be able to get her out of her room—and maybe have her join the celebration for Sarah's birthday. Perhaps she needed to be reunited with those she trusted.

Sarah, Miles, Joan, and the other patients were enjoying their time in the sun. It was a crisp comfortable fall day. In a few weeks, it would be time for coats and getting ready for the snow. They all sat on a big blanket, and Miles made origami animals for the two women. He liked to make them and found it relaxing. When he was in college, crafting them eased the stress before tests. Sarah loved all the different colors he used when making them. Joan was just content to see their smiling faces.

Dr. Katz went in to talk to Phoebe. He found her sitting against the wall with her knees pulled her to her chest, smiling shyly as he came over to sit beside her. "Good afternoon, Phoebe. Are you feeling any better?"

She nodded and rested her chin on her knees.

"That's good. It's important that we get you back to your old self again. Sometimes we have bad days, and I think that's all that happened to you—just one big, old bad day. I think it'd help you a lot if you joined the others today. I think that would be a great present for Sarah. We may have to give you something that will make you a little sleepy, but you can join everyone for the party. I know you'll enjoy that.

She looked at him and scrunched up her face. She did not like the way the medicines made her feel, but she missed everyone so badly. Being cooped up in that room reminded her of where her parents used to keep her, and she did not want to stay in there for another minute. She agreed to the medication.

"That's good, Phoebe. We'll get you your shot—and then get you all cleaned up before you go see everybody."

Nurse Gabrielle came in and held her hand while Dr. Katz gave her a Valium. It was not enough to make her extremely groggy, but it was enough to keep her relaxed so she could enjoy herself. His plan was to try to get her back into her old room that night and back to her original routine. Keeping her in that room any longer was going to do nothing but remind her of trauma.

After everyone had gone back inside, they decided to pass the time before the party by watching *Casablanca*. Sarah sat beside Miles, and their hands touched for a brief moment, making her smile and Miles blush. They looked to each other and then back to the movie, letting their hands stay brushed together the whole while. Gabrielle had Phoebe showered, washing her, drying her off, and getting her dressed. She looked better when she was all cleaned up in her tan capris and orange sweater.

Gabrielle took time to brush out her blonde hair, taking extra care to make sure it was just right before pulling it up into a ponytail. She helped the wobbly Phoebe back into her wheelchair and smiled. "There we go. Don't you look so very pretty, Miss Phoebe. I just know everyone will be so glad to see you."

Dr. Katz was optimistic about how well Phoebe would handle her social group again.

Carrie got off of the elevator. Dr. Katz saw her and said, "Ah, Carrie. Did you enjoy your days off?"

"Yes, I did. Thank you. So how excited is Sarah today?" She chuckled.

"I believe excited would be a gross understatement. I was just on my way to pick up her birthday present. Care to join me?"

Carrie nodded and followed him down the hall.

Gabrielle was standing in front of the shower room, and Phoebe was waiting in a chair.

Carrie smiled from ear to ear and rushed over to give Phoebe a hug.

"Oh, sweetheart. You look great. It's so good to see you." She looked over her shoulder at Dr. Katz. "Sarah is going to be thrilled to see her. You think she's up for this?"

"Well, I did medicate her to keep her calm. I'm hoping that we can get her back to her own room tonight." He took the chair from Gabrielle.

They walked to the TV room, excited to see Sarah's reaction when they brought her a present. Carrie peeked through the doorway to see Sarah, Miles, and Joan watching a movie.

Dr. Katz smiled and put a hand on Phoebe's shoulder. "You're going to be fine," he whispered, more to himself than anyone, before they wheeled her in. "Surprise, Sarah. Happy birthday!"

Sarah squealed with delight and practically beamed as she jetted across the room and threw her arms around Phoebe. Joan was on the verge of tears. Miles was also very happy to see her—and not just because he was worried. Having her there made Sarah all the more happy, and her happiness was so very important to him.

"Oh my word," Sarah squeaked. "Phoebe, I have missed you so much."

Carrie watched with a warm smile as Sarah practically squeezed the stuffing out of poor Phoebe.

"Dr. Katz?" Sarah looked up at him. "Does Phoebe have to go right back to the room after the party is over?"

He smiled at her. "Well, Sarah, I was thinking maybe it would be better for her if she tried coming back out here and joining the group. Do you think you'd like that for a birthday present?"

Sarah held Phoebe's hands as she looked up and nodded. "That would be wonderful."

"Now, Sarah, I want you to know that if Phoebe is going to stay out here, then it would be best for everyone if she were on her medications to make sure she remains calm."

Sarah's frown curved into a pout. "Phoebe didn't mean to hurt that cop. He must not have been a very nice man," she said.

"Sarah," Miles said, "I don't think the doctor is trying to blame Phoebe. He just wants to make sure that she doesn't get upset and have to leave us and go to the quiet room again."

"That's right," Carrie said. "We're just trying to do what's best for Phoebe."

Sarah nodded; she was just happy to have her friend back. If she had anything to say about it, they would never be apart again.

Dr. Katz left Phoebe in their care once she was comfortable and went off to do his sessions for the day.

Carrie sat with the group for a few minutes before going inside to see Elaine. When she walked into Elaine's room, Elaine was sleeping. She looked like the lightest nudge would wake her. "Hey girl, I just wanted to come in and sit with you for a bit. I have some good news for you." She pulled up a seat. "Phoebe came out of the quiet room today, and the doctor is going to try to let her stay out with everyone else. They really miss you, but I know you'll wake up when you're ready. I don't know what happened with Kyle, but I know it wasn't your fault. I promise I'll be here to help you sort everything out when you wake up." She lowered her head with a sigh and began to pray, something she had not done in many years. She concentrated on a prayer for Elaine to come back soon, and she felt Elaine squeeze her hand twice. Her eyes widened as she looked at her, tears welling up. She wanted to believe that this was her way of saying that she was still there and that she was trying for them. She wanted to run and tell them all, but she didn't want to get their hopes up. After all, it could have been a muscle spasm. Today was Sarah's day, and after the party, she would take Dr. Katz aside and talk to him about it. For now, there was a party to set up.

The day was filled with excitement, and everyone was busy helping. Carrie was putting up the streamers and inflating balloons. Joan was hanging the banner she had made with Sarah. Sarah was talking to Phoebe about the origami animals. She placed two of them in her lap: a blue and a red one.

Phoebe loved the colors and was glad that Sarah let her hold one.

Miles decided to read poetry for a while in his room. He was about to start reading when something caught the corner of his eye. Gina—as grotesque as ever—was shushing him and standing in front of the closet. He slowly set his book down, keeping his eyes trained on her. She slowly moved across the floor and then out into the hall. He followed closely behind her and the bloody footprint she was leaving in her wake. He watched in fear as she moved undetected over to the group. Sarah was laughing happily and playing with a piece of streamer beside Joan. Gina slithered around Sarah, pretending to stroke her hair before she brought her hand up to Sarah's throat and made a swift slicing motion.

"No!" Miles screamed, startling the group.

Gina sped down the hallway.

"What's wrong, Miles?" Sarah asked. "You don't like the decorations?"

He stood in silence for a moment as his eyes darted around, finding Joan on the ladder. He cleared his throat and laughed nervously. "Of course I do. Sorry. I didn't mean to give anybody a start. I just thought Joan was about to fall for a second." He crossed the room to the ladder and helped her down. "Let me get that for you," he said before he straightened out the banner.

"Thank you, Miles. That's kind of you to help," Joan said.

Miles's eyes crept back toward the door. A shiver jumped up his spine. He took a few deep breaths and tried to remain calm. After all, it was Sarah's day—and he wasn't about to spoil it by running about like a raving lunatic.

CHAPTER 12

After dinner, everyone migrated to the crafts room, which had been transformed for the party.

Miles took a small detour to his room to collect the gift he'd made for Sarah.

Carrie brought out the cake and the ice cream, Joan poured the punch, and Gabrielle stacked the presents.

Sarah was absolutely glowing. She felt like she was floating on the air. Other than Christmas, her birthday was her absolute favorite time of year.

Miles returned just in time to sing "Happy Birthday" with everyone. Dr. Katz joined in at the end. He had checked on Elaine and was thrilled to have seen her try to squeeze his hand. He knew she was trying to come around; he felt it in his heart. He wanted to tell the others, but he did not want to take any of the glory away from Sarah's birthday.

Gabrielle cut the cake and made sure everyone had a piece.

Sarah was elated to have chocolate cake, but she hated to see such a beautiful thing get chopped up. It looked like a cute basket full of icing sunflowers. The cake had been a roaring success, and everyone was pleased to hear that there was plenty for them all to have seconds.

When the cake and ice cream plates were cleaned up, it was time to play games. Sarah's favorites were pin the tail on the donkey and guessing the number of jellybeans in a big mason jar. When it was time to open her presents, she sat down beside Phoebe.

Joan passed the presents to her. The first she opened was a new diary with puppies on it. It came with a nice pen set that the staff had all chipped in for. Carrie got her a new pair of blue Keds since Sarah liked hers. Joan had painted a beautiful watercolor portrait of Sarah sitting on a big blanket under the oak tree with Tobbie in her arms.

Sarah's eyes got teary. "Oh, Joan. Thank you. Thank you so much. I can't wait to hang it in my room. It's beautiful." Sarah gave Joan a hug.

"You're so very welcome, sweet girl." Joan smiled. "I'm so glad that you like it."

Sarah cooed over some homemade, glitter-covered gifts from the patients before it was time for Miles's gift. He was trying to keep his hands from shaking as he handed her a long, skinny box with a red ribbon. She held the box carefully in her lap, carefully removed the ribbon, and lifted the lid with care.

She gasped when she saw the contents of the box. It was the most beautiful, thoughtful present she had every received—aside from Tobbie, of course. Wrapped in tissue paper, there were twelve little roses made from clay and painted the prettiest shade of red she'd ever seen. The stems were made of popsicle sticks, split down the middle, and painted green. Tears of joy ran down her cheeks as she looked up at Miles. "They're gorgeous. They must have taken you forever to get them done. I can't even begin to tell you what this means to me—that you would make me something so very special for my birthday. Thank you, Miles."

He lowered his head with a weak smile. "I would have gotten you real ones if I could."

She shook her head and held the box tightly. "No, no. These are better than real ones. Real ones shrivel and die. These I can continue to keep forever—ones I can treasure."

Everyone wanted to get a closer look at the special roses. Sarah let them all look, but no one could touch them.

Carrie leaned against Miles with a chuckle and a bright smile. "You did great. Just look at her. You made her day extra special. She's over the moon." She exchanged a knowing, sweet glance with him before she went over to peek at the special gift.

When bedtime rolled around, everyone was pretty tired out.

Sarah was still on cloud nine, barely able to keep still in line to get her medication. After collecting them, she gathered up all her presents carefully and took them to her room. She carefully put the roses on Elaine's bed while she made room for them on her dresser. "You guys will look absolutely perfect up here. Oh, Tobbie, wait till I show you what Miles made for my birthday. You'll love them." She giggled and spun around to look for Tobbie. He was usually on her bed. She took a deep breath and frowned. "Maybe you fell under the bed?" She got down on her knees, lifted her covers, and peered under her bed. Nothing! Tobbie was nowhere to be seen. *This is terrible. Tobbie is missing.* She felt like she couldn't breathe. She frantically looked under Elaine's bed, finding nothing. *This is impossible. He has to be here.* She pulled everything out of the closet, but her search bore no fruit. She bolted out to the nurse's station, running into Carrie.

Carrie's eyes widened, and she grabbed Sarah's shoulders. "Sarah, sweetheart, what's wrong?"

Sarah's lower lip quivered before she let out a loud cry and burst into tears.

"Sarah, please take a deep breath and tell me what's wrong."

Joan and Miles came rushing over. "Carrie, what's wrong with Sarah?" Joan asked.

"I don't know. I can't get her to calm down long enough to tell me."

Miles put his hand on her arm and frowned. "Sarah? Hey, listen. It's okay. It's gonna be okay. Just take a deep breath and try to tell us what's wrong."

Sarah coughed and said, "Tobbie's gone! Somebody took him! He's not in my room, under the beds, the closet, nowhere! Someone took him! Why would someone do that? Please help me! Help me find him! He's scared when he's alone. We have to hurry!"

"Okay, sweetheart," Carrie said. "Everything's going to be fine. He has to be somewhere."

Miles wiped her face with his hand and tucked her hair behind her ear. "Just try to stay calm. He can't have gone far. Maybe you left him some—"

"No!" Sarah screamed, pulling away from him. "I put him on the bed where I put him every single day. He's gone! Someone stole him!"

A small group of patients volunteered to look for Tobbie.

Dr. Katz went into the TV room to talk to Sarah.

When Sarah saw him, she sprang up and ran to him. "Dr. Katz, it's an emergency! A tragedy! Tobbie's been dognapped! We have to find him!"

"We will find him, but it's important that you try to stay calm."

While the patients checked the other rooms, the doctor and Miles stayed tried to keep Sarah calm.

Carrie and Joan went off to ask the other patients if they'd seen the stuffed toy.

Miles held Sarah's hand and attempted to keep her from panicking again. Seeing her in so much pain broke his heart, and he told her to stay calm and with the doctor. He was going to check all the garbage cans and all the bathrooms.

Dr. Katz was at an absolute loss. He couldn't think of anyone who would do such a cruel thing to her. They all knew how much Tobbie meant to her.

Miles was unsuccessful in locating him and looked absolutely crushed

Dr. Katz sent the other patients back to bed, promising to continue the search in the morning.

Carrie and Joan came into the room. Carrie's hands were behind her back, and she had a devastated expression.

"Did you find Tobbie?" Sarah's fragile heart was wavering.

Joan said, "Yes. We found Tobbie, but there's something we need to tell you, sweetheart."

Her face lit up. "Oh, you found him? Please give him to me. Oh, thank you. Thank you!" She smiled.

Carrie looked as if her heart would break. She sighed and brought her hands from behind her back.

Sarah gasped. Somebody had ripped off Tobbie's head. Sarah clutched the pieces and held him to her chest. Her sobs broke the hearts of everyone in the room. What had she ever done to anyone to deserve something like this? Who would do this? She was devastated.

"Who the hell would do this to Sarah?" Miles snapped and balled his fists.

"Where did you find him?" Dr. Katz asked.

"Well, that's where it's complicated," Carrie said.

"What do you mean? Where was Tobbie?" the doctor demanded.

"Well," Joan said slowly, "we're very sorry to say that we found Tobbie on the floor of Miles's closet."

Miles's eyes were blown wide in shock. "Wait a minute. That can't be right! There's no way that he was in my room! I'd never do such a horrible thing, especially to Sarah!"

Dr. Katz raised a hand. "Miles, no one is accusing you of doing this. Do you have any idea how Tobbie could have gotten into your closet?"

Miles choked on panic and tears. "Sarah, please. You have to believe me! Someone had to have put him there! I would never do anything like that to hurt you. I know how important he is to you."

She turned away and asked Carrie to escort her to her room.

"Sarah, please don't be upset with me. I swear that I didn't do it!"

"Don't ever talk to me again! I hate you!" Sarah slapped him hard enough to send him reeling to the ground.

Dr. Katz took Sarah to her room with Joan.

Carrie dropped to her knees beside Miles and put her arms around him. "Miles, Sarah didn't mean that. She's just upset right now. That's all." She rubbed his back.

"I swear I'd never hurt Tobbie—ever. I don't know how he got into my closet!"

She frowned and held him tighter. "I know—and I believe you. I know that Sarah knows that too. She couldn't possibly believe you did something like that."

"I knew she was upset with the time I spent with Sarah, but I never thought that she'd do something this cruel."

"Miles, you know who did it?" Carrie leaned back and held his shoulders, looking down at him. "Tell me please!"

He shook his head. "It's not that simple. You'd never believe me. Nobody would ever believe me. I know it. You'd think I'm crazy like Dr. Katz does."

"Miles, I promise to believe you. Just tell me so we can help Sarah and everyone else understand."

He looked up at her before looking toward the door, swallowing once. "It … it was Gina."

Carrie blinked. "Your dead fiancée?"

"Yeah. She was angry about the time we'd been spending … she came out of my room today and pretended to slit Sarah's throat. That's why I ended up screaming. She's been coming to me every night. I've been awake. I know it. I swear to you it was her!"

"All right, Miles. It's going to be all right. I believe you. We'll let everything calm down overnight, and we will go talk to Dr. Katz about it in the morning."

Miles fell silent, gritting his teeth. He knew she did not believe him, but he was exhausted. He stomped back to his room without saying anything to her or anyone else on the way.

That night, Joan listened to Sarah's sobs through the wall. She knew that Miles would have never done something like that to anyone—let alone sweet Sarah. A tear fell down her cheek as she shut her eyes tightly and pressed her palms together. She prayed over and over for all the people in her life who she cherished and cared for.

Carrie sat in her vehicle, keys hanging freely in the ignition, and thought about what Miles had said to her. He appeared to be crazy by saying that kind of thing, but she could not understand it. He was doing so well, and he never exhibited that kind of behavior. An aching feeling that would not be ignored was tugging at her stomach, and she felt as though something was missing. When she couldn't think about it any longer, she drove away from the crazy of Willow Tree and back toward the normal of home.

Miles tossed and turned in his bed. He was pissed and heartbroken, unable to sleep. He listened to Sarah crying her eyes out down the hall. Gina had done it. She had to be the one, but he couldn't find a way to make everyone believe it—no matter how hard he tried. *She was real!* He damned her in his mind, wondering how she could do that to someone so kind. He let out a frustrated yell and chucked his pillow toward the closet. It flew past Gina's face as she materialized before him. She looked clean and smelled sweetly of lavender.

"Miles, please don't be angry with me, sweetheart."

He sat up in bed, turned the light on, and gave her a dirty look. "Get out of here, Gina. I don't want to ever see you around again."

She just gave him a smile and came toward the bed. "Darling, you don't really mean that, do you?"

He pushed away from her and against the wall. "You bet your ass I mean it. What you did to Sarah and me was unforgivable. Tobbie meant everything to her. You destroyed one of the only things that brought her comfort—and you blamed it on me. They think I did it."

"Don't be angry, Miles. It's just a stupid toy—and she needed to learn a lesson!"

"Why the hell would she need a lesson?"

"Because you belong to me, and that woman is trying to take you away."

Miles wanted to be so angry with her, but she was wearing the red V-neck sweater he'd gotten her for their last Christmas together. She also wore the brown suede skirt she'd felt so badly about him buying. He looked into her soft brown eyes, which he'd dreamed about so often, as she climbed into bed beside him. He could feel her soft skin against his.

Gina started to caress his body, and Miles let out a slight moan. He tried to move away, knowing that somewhere in his mind he was positive this was insane, but Gina was so beautiful and sweet—just the way he'd remembered. He was trying to stay angry with her because he knew he loved Sarah—and he'd loved Sarah for a long time. What Gina had done to her was evil and unforgivable. He did love Gina, but it was not the same anymore. His mind was getting cloudy as she started to stroke the inside of his thigh.

"Miles, no one will ever love you the way I do," she cooed into his ear. "Did you see their faces? None of them believe you. Sarah told you she hated you. I've never said such a terrible thing to you."

His head fell back, and he shut his eyes.

"See, baby? It's me you still love. Listen, I want you to come with me—to be together again, forever, never to be parted. Don't you want that?"

Miles loved Sarah, but Gina was here with him again, asking him to come away with her. She was really there, and she'd forgiven him for what he had done.

"They don't love you," she purred. "They hurt you by thinking you were a liar. Understand? And they have to be taught a lesson too." She was sending him to new heights with her touch; the last time he'd felt like that was the last time they were in bed together as a couple. "Miles, we need to be together. Don't you want to be with me?"

Miles's heart was racing, and he found it difficult to breathe.

"I want to be with you, Miles!"

"Gina, I want to be with you, but what you did to Sarah was wrong. She's a sweet girl, and what you did was terrible."

She squeezed him, causing Miles to wince in pain.

"Gina, that hurts." He felt sick to his stomach. "Gina, that hurts. Please stop. You have to stop. I can't—."

"No," she growled. "You have to see how these people really think of you. Close your eyes and see, Miles."

He didn't want to see, but something was forcing their faces into his mind. Looks of disgust and disappointment glared at him. They shook their heads and turned away. He saw Sarah in her bed. She was crying and looking more scared and alone than he'd ever seen. He started to weep quietly, shaking his head, wanting nothing more than for this to disappear and the pain to leave him.

"Just say the word, Miles," Gina cooed again. "I can make it all go away—and then we can be together. Don't you want that?" She stroked his hair as he opened his eyes and looked up at her. "Shh, baby. Don't cry." She wiped his eyes with her free hand. "Everything's going to be fine. I will take care of you. You want us to be free, don't you?" She stroked him more gently.

"See? Doesn't that feel nice?"

Miles wanted all the pain to go away. She'd never lied to him. He realized they all hated him. If Sarah had really loved him, she would have believed him instead of yelling and humiliating him.

"They have to pay, Miles. You know that, right?" she whispered.

"How can I be with you?" he whimpered.

She kissed his forehead. "Shh. Tomorrow, Miles, we will finally be free. The detective will help. You just have to do what I say."

"He'll help us?" he asked.

She smiled and kissed him gently on the lips. "He is the key, love. Miles, I need to know that you want this."

"Yes! I want this, Gina. I want you. Please no more pain. Take it away!" he shouted.

Gina crawled on top of him, and swiftly they were entwined as he came to his nirvana. His breathing steadied, he opened his eyes to see her beautiful face, and his eyes widened.

A hideous creature had taken her place. It was on his chest and had gray skin and black eyes. She smiled with her jagged teeth and dug her nails into his stomach.

Miles's mouth opened to scream, but the creature crawled into his mouth and down his throat, forcing him onto his side. He held his gut, fell out of bed, and scrambled to the bathroom. He fell to his knees in front of the toilet. He was having a hard time trying to breathe between fits of violent vomiting. After a couple minutes of clinging to the side of the toilet, he shakily made his way over to the sink and splashed cold water on his face. His body felt like it was no longer his own.

When he looked into the mirror, his face was unrecognizable. He almost couldn't believe that he was looking in the same mirror. His eyes were dark, and his skin was gray and clammy. He turned away from the creature that captured his gaze and shuffled back to bed in a trance. He was aware that he was no longer in control of his body.

His last passing thought before sleep was about the detective and his ability to liberate him.

Cinder cooed silently. It was Miles's time to pay for being so bad.

CHAPTER 13

While everyone was enjoying the party, Detective Eubanks made his way to the childhood home of Elaine Cooper to speak with her mother. He wanted to get some insight into this woman who everyone was sure wasn't a killer. They were covering for her. He knew she'd had a turbulent childhood and a few minor scrapes with the law when she was a teenager, but he was most intrigued about the mysterious circumstances under which her father had passed away. Mary Cooper had testified that Elaine was an extremely troublesome child, but he wanted to discuss it in person.

He kept looking over at the map. The farm was out in the middle of nowhere. They lived like hermits. When he finally came upon the family home, it hardly seemed like one. It was a gloomy, one-story home that looked like it had once been white. It was in desperate need of a serious paint job. He parked next to a rusted out pickup truck that was propped up on cinderblocks. It didn't look like it had moved in quite some time.

The porch felt like it could collapse at any second. It creaked loudly when he pulled back the screen door, hanging on one hinge, and knocked loudly on the door a few times. He let the screen close and took a step back. After a moment, he could hear shuffling behind the door.

A woman of at least sixty-five opened the door. She had gray, short, curly hair and a heavily stained muumuu, a scowl for the ages, and a cigarette. She blew smoke his way and said, "Yeah? Who are you—and what the hell are ya on my property for? Whatever yer sellin', I don't want." She moved to slam the door.

"No, Miss Cooper. I'm not here to sell you anything. This is about your daughter. I'm Detective Eubanks, and I was wondering if it was possible to have a moment of your time."

She cocked a brow and looked him up and down. "And what the hell for? She's locked up over in Pennsylvania. Did she escape or something? 'Cuz this is the last place she'd go, hon." She opened the screen and flicked the butt of her cigarette into the dirt before looking back at him.

"No, ma'am. She hasn't, but she certainly isn't doing well. Can I come in and discuss it with you?"

She stared at him for a moment before she leaned back against the door-frame. "Who died?" she asked.

"Excuse me?" He raised his brow.

"Well, someone must've died. Why else would you pedal your ass all the way out here and wanna talk 'bout Elaine?"

"There was an incident at Willow Tree, and your daughter may have been involved. However, I am terribly sorry to inform you that Elaine has slipped into a coma."

"That so? Ya don't say."

He took a step toward the door. "Could I please come in? It'll only take a minute."

"Ah, to hell with it. Yeah, come on in and have a seat." She stepped out of the doorway and gestured to a faded chair that looked like it might have been green at one time. The front room was covered with books, aging newspapers, magazines, and dirty dishes. There was a putrid odor; not one place was untouched by grime and filth.

Detective Eubanks was unsure of when these rooms had last seen the light of day—or if they ever had. He reluctantly took a seat on the couch opposite of it.

Mary Cooper took her seat in the chair, kicking up a small cloud of what he hoped was dust. He guessed it was a combination of dirt and God knows what else. She took another cigarette from the pack, took a long drag, and focused on him. "Now, what was it you wanted again, Detective?"

"I read through each of the police reports filed on Elaine and spoke with those involved in her arrest at the motel. Am I correct in hearing that you testified for the state at Elaine's trial?" He did not want his back to touch the couch. He attempted to not let any part of himself come into contact with it.

"Yep. People needed to know the truth 'bout that girl."

"Mrs. Cooper, you are her mother. Didn't you find that just the slightest bit difficult?"

"Now you listen here, Detective." She put her cigarette down in the full ashtray on the end table. "I wasn't one of those women that actually wanted to have damn kids, and I ain't never had that maternal instinct. Trust me, I wasn't a happy person when I found out my old man got me knocked up, and neither was he for that matter, but the whole family and friends were excited, so we thought the hell with it. I thought maybe by the time she was born, I'd feel something, but nope. I was miserable that whole nine months and even more so when the shit was born. Nothin' but trouble, I tell ya. Always crying. She had what they call the colic, sometimes just screamin' her head off for hours. It got so bad I had to put her in the basket in the back of her closet just to get some damn quiet around here. Then when she got to walkin' around, gettin' into absolutely everything, breakin' shit, climbin' around. I thought that when she got older, she'd learn to keep her hands off my things, but no, things just got worse.

"When she was four, she started havin' all kinds of nightmares, just screamin' at all hours of the night every damn day. I finally had to break down and buy a stupid light for the room so she could keep it on, run up my bill on her silly-ass dreams. That was about the time she got strange as hell." She rested her elbow on the arm of the chair and looked off in thought, resting her cheek on her knuckles.

"Like how, Mrs. Cooper?"

"Let's see. She didn't have many friends, kept to herself mostly. I'd find her talkin' to herself, and that's when she started in with the stealin' and the lyin'. I'd find my jewelry in her room, and she'd get a spankin'. She'd shout, 'Momma I didn't do it,' but who the hell was it then? Some imaginary friend she had to make 'cuz she couldn't make any real ones? An' I told her that if she didn't stop with the lyin', she'd go to bed without supper. She went to bed many a night without supper, but it just didn't keep her outta trouble."

"So Elaine had trouble when she was young?" He wasn't sure the blame was all on the child. Anyone would need therapy after having to live with this woman for eighteen years.

"Problems would've been simple, Detective." She sighed. "She was an unholy terror. When Wayne got little Judy to babysit for us so he and I could go raise hell and get a drink, Elaine decided to go play dress up in all my good church dresses. Judy told 'er to put 'em up. Well, apparently, Elaine didn't like that, and she calls us up at the bar and tells us we have to come home quick 'cuz Judy's hurt."

He leaned forward and put his hands on his elbows. "What happened to her?" he asked.

"Ah, to hell if I know. She said she fell asleep, and some crazy creature-lookin' thing attacked her and tried to choke her. We found her in the closet, screaming about this and that, welts and scratches all over her throat. Doctors said she must've done it to herself durin' a nightmare and freaked out, but I knew better. I knew that Elaine was lying when she said she was asleep when it happened and didn't know anything. I found my good church dress all slashed up on the closet floor." She reached for her cigarette, but it had burned itself down to the filter. She growled under her breath, picked it up, and smothered it in the ashes.

"So you're telling me that Elaine would do things and blame them on some-one else?"

"It was always that damn imaginary friend she'd made up. That's who she'd always be blamin'. She was the most ungrateful child I'd ever known. The day she turned eighteen, she came into the kitchen, suitcase packed, and with barely a hundred dollars she got from workin' at the Dairy Queen over the summer, she announced that she was gone. And out the door she went. No good-bye. That was the last I saw of her until about three years ago. She showed up and asked if she could stay a few nights. She was on her way to California. Wayne wouldn't let her in though till she promised she wasn't pregnant or hidin' from the law. Said she was just passin' through. How do ya like that shit? Passin' through." She scowled. "Passin' through my ass. Where Elaine was, there was always trouble, and her visit was no exception."

Eubanks pushed up off his elbows and clasped his hands together. "Mrs. Cooper, I know this may be hard, but if you wouldn't mind, I'd like it if you could tell me about the day your husband died."

She leaned back in her chair and exhaled loudly. "Saddest damn day of my life was the day I lost Wayne—and the day after Elaine came home. We were sittin' down to breakfast, and Wayne was getting ready to clean the gutters. And then … Elaine just apologized for everything. You coulda knocked me over with a feather. Wayne got up and left without a word. We didn't speak, but

Elaine helped me out with the dishes and went outside. I guess she was going to talk to him, but a few minutes later, I heard her screaming. I ran outside and … my poor Wayne was impaled on our gatepost. She ran inside, covering her mouth. We didn't speak for days. We had guests over after the burial, and in front of God and everyone in that room, she took my hands, apologized for my loss, and walked out with her suitcase. I hadn't seen her again since I was called to testify against her."

She narrowed her eyes as she looked over at him. "I know in my heart that Elaine killed my husband and got away with it, no question, and I'll tell ya, I jumped at the chance to say my piece in court and have that murderer finally thrown away to the wolves of justice—somewhere she couldn't hurt anyone ever again. That girl is pure evil, and that coma is God's way of making her pay for her sins! Yeah, she plays the victim, all innocent and pretty, but that's how she'll get ya." She lowered her eyes and folded her hands in her lap.

Eubanks got to his feet and discreetly brushed off the back of his slacks. "Mrs. Cooper, I know I've already taken up quite a bit of your time, but I'd really like to take a look at Elaine's room. Would you mind that? I promise I won't be but a moment."

She nodded and rubbed her temples. "Yeah. Second door on the right—the one with the tulip on it."

He thanked her and walked to the bedroom. Never in his life had he seen a room so depressing: a twin-sized wrought-iron bed that looked like it was on its last leg, a dreary, cheap, wooden nightstand, and a lamp with a blue duck as its base. The lampshade was falling off to one side, and it was covered in moth-bitten holes.

There were no frills and no pretty dresser to place pretty, girly things. There were no cute pictures on the wall or posters of boy bands or movies. It was a depressing atmosphere. The curtains that hung over the wall had been white and yellow gingham, but they were faded beyond belief and rotting right off the rod. Three tattered dolls were in the corner below the window. One was missing an arm, another a leg, and the third's eye was busted out of the socket. The room was starting to creep him out the longer he examined it.

The closet doors were left askew. He peeked inside, but it was too dark. He removed his penlight and his handkerchief, using it as a barrier between him and anything in the room. He shined the light into the closet and pried the door open with little difficulty. It felt like it could come right off in his grasp. On the shelves, he found a few old blankets and some empty wire coat hangers. On the floor, a small box held a coloring book missing half its pages, a box of busted crayons, and a journal. He picked the journal up and flipped it to the first page.

Entry 1

Today Momma accused me of taking her stupid seashell clips. I don't even like them, but she said she found them under my pillow. I told her I didn't do it, but she didn't believe me. She never does. She made me go down to the basement again, even though I begged and begged her. She just dragged me by my hair for being too slow and put me in the big cabinet again. The metal was cold on my bare feet. I'm glad Cinder was there with me—even though she's the one who keeps taking all of Momma's stuff and doing bad things. I keep asking her not to because I'm the one who always gets in trouble for it. It isn't fair. My stomach really hurts. Momma said no dinner again because liars don't deserve food.

I have to go now. She doesn't know I have this. Sally, a girl in my class, left this journal behind in her desk when she moved away. I tore out all the used pages. Her life was pretty boring anyway. Momma always says it's not stealing if a person leaves it behind.
Love,
Elaine and Cinder

Detective Eubanks slowly closed the journal with a light sigh, shoving the journal into his pocket. If she didn't know about it, then she wouldn't really be upset about him taking it. Besides, it was Elaine's—and like she said, it wasn't stealing if someone had left it behind.

He moved to stand up, and his penlight caught something in the corner. He leaned in for a closer look, having to get further into the closet than anticipated, finding it much deeper than it seemed. His eyes widened at the startling image. *Jesus Christ! What the fuck is that?*

On the wall, there was a crayon drawing of a startlingly eerie face of a young girl, but it looked more like a creature than a child. His penlight passed over stringy black hair, big black eyes, jagged teeth, and red mouth. He was not sure what it meant until his eyes drifted down to find, drawn in red, what looked to be a tongue farther down. He could imagine Elaine sitting there, angrily scribbling into the wall with so much rage.

He had seen his share of shit, but this closet was making him sick to his stomach. He wanted nothing more than to be out of this house. He wanted to look at one more thing before he left—to confirm the things in Elaine's journal.

Mary was resting comfortably and thumbing through a magazine. "Find anything interesting, Detective?" she asked.

"No not really, but Elaine's room looks rather childish. You said she left when she was eighteen? She never wanted to change anything?"

"What the hell for? I wasn't about to let her crowd the room with all that crap teenagers thought they needed. She was damn lucky to have what she did. She didn't need no spoilin'."

He couldn't imagine what it had been like for Elaine to live in that dreary room, but it seemed like she spent more time in the basement than she did up there anyways. "Mrs. Cooper, I know this may sound odd, but would you mind me looking around your basement?"

She looked up at him again and took a long drag of her cigarette. "What the hell for? I don't give a rat's ass. Knock yourself out. Go through the kitchen, but be careful. The steps are loose. I about broke my neck last time I went down there. There's a bunch of Wayne's old junk down there, so mind your step."

He made it through the copious piles of crap Mary had stacked up around everything. He tried the basement door, and a loud clunk came from the door as he failed to pull it open,

"You've gotta give it a good yank!" Mary shouted before she turned on a televangelist's show on the TV.

Eubanks nearly lost his footing as pulled the door free of the frame. He reached for the light chain and pulled it to let the harshness of the naked bulb pour over the stairs. He descended slowly and with the upmost care so as not to disturb the fragile structure. When he had reached the bottom of the stairs, he spied a metal cabinet against the wall behind a pile of junk. The light barely reached that corner of the basement. He turned on to the penlight and looked at the cabinet. The key was still hanging in the handle.

Fearful of what he would find, he turned the key. The lock clicked, and the

heavy doors opened slowly. A horrific smell forced him to gag. He brought up
his sleeve to cover his nose and mouth, shining a light into the cabinet. The
floor of it was covered in old urine stains, but he was astonished to find that
there was barely enough room for a large toddler underneath the bottom shelf.
He noticed something peculiar. Deep scratches across the front of the cabinet
were much too deep to have been made by a child. Elaine would have lost her
fingernails and stained the doors in blood by the time she did damage like that.
Something was locked in there, and it was desperate in its attempts to get out.
His stomach churned, and he shoved the cabinet shut, making his way out of
the basement as carefully—and as quickly—as possible.

When he returned to the living room, Mrs. Cooper looked up from her
program.

"Mrs. Cooper, did you have something locked up in that cabinet downstairs?"

She leaned back and set her remote down. "Not a something detective—a
someone."

He thought he would choke, not having thought in a million years this
woman would openly admit it to him. "Elaine?" he asked.

"Oh yeah, when she'd lie or steal. God, the echo was terrible though, listenin'
to her just scream and wail that she didn't do anything, just scream and scream
till she'd lose her voice."

"So you'd take her down to the basement and just lock her up in that cabinet?" His eyes were wide, and his head was cocked to the side.

"Yeah? What of it? That's what I said, didn't I? She needed a firm hand—and
spankin' her wasn't cuttin' it." She folded her arms.

"Does the name Cinder mean anything?" he asked.

Her arms snapped down to the chair as she sat up. Her face turned red,
and pointed at him. "Who the hell told you about that? She wasn't nobody—just
a stupid-ass excuse she made up when she was a kid! What? She spoutin' off
and blaming shit on her again up there in crazy town?" She settled back in her
chair, arms tucked together.

"I think we're done here. I won't take up anymore of your time, ma'am." He
made his way to the door, not able to get out of here quick enough.

"Detective, when my girl wakes up, tell her to at least write her mother on
her birthday." Her cackling sent her into a fit of coughs. When she caught her
breath, he made a swift exit.

Back in his car, he was having the toughest time wrapping his head around any of it. He was sure Dr. Katz would want in on some of this information. He flipped open his phone and dialed as he tore down the road. He wanted to get as much distance between the house and his car as he could. He left a message that he would be in to see the doctor in the morning. He tossed his phone down on the passenger seat. It was already late. He headed straight home for some food, a cold beer, and a shower. After being in that house, he definitely needed one.

CHAPTER 14

It was very late by the time Eubanks arrived home. He took Elaine's journal out of his jacket and tossed it on his coffee table with his car keys. He decided on a shower before eating anything. He fished a pair of boxers from his laundry basket and smelled them once, determining they had passed the test for cleanliness. He took them, his Chicago Bears T-shirt, and a pair of blue gym shorts in to the bathroom. After he was showered and dressed, he raked his hands through his wet hair and sighed. *Good enough for now.* He shuffled into his kitchen, gulping down his first beer as he pan-fried a steak.

It was all such a mystery, and Elaine was the biggest enigma of all. He was reviewing his facts. Elaine had been in that room with Kyle when he was murdered, and he had died the exact same way that Bryce Freeman had died, which Elaine had also been present for. Of course, there were the names Phoebe had scrawled all over her walls. What was their connection to these murders? Perhaps Elaine had confessed to Phoebe, thinking her secrets were safe with her?

He rubbed his arm where the stitches were starting to itch and growled quietly to himself. The itching was irritating him. He was also confused at everyone's insistence that Phoebe was a docile person, but he knew firsthand that she could be violent. The victim in her latched her teeth onto him. Elaine was definitely the ringleader in all of this—as far as he was concerned—and he couldn't understand why the staff was covering for her. He hoped she would hurry up and wake up so he could get some answers out of her.

He devoured his steak and polished off his third beer before cracking open her journal. He wanted sleep, but he needed to read more of her journal first.

Entry 2
Today Momma was outside working in the flower garden again. I wanted to help so I went and got Daddy's little shovel and went on to be with her. She was planting more of her favorite flowers. She loves marigolds. I asked if I could help, but she shouted no at me and told me never to dig in her garden, ever. She said I could help by getting lost, that it would help her a lot. I don't understand. Momma's always so mean to me.
—Elaine

Entry 3
My tummy hurts … I'm so hungry today. Momma put me in the cabinet again. I wanted to surprise her. I thought it'd be helpful to finish up planting all the flowers for her. She came out and hit me across the face with the back of her hand. I cried, and she made me go back to the metal cabinet. I was bad again. I hate being bad. I hate the cabinet even more. It's so very hot in there. I cried for a long, long time, and Cinder wouldn't stop scratching at the door. We couldn't catch our breath at all in the heat, and I had to pee so badly. Momma wouldn't let us out. I peed myself … Daddy came and let me out when it was dark and carried me to bed, but Momma said I smelled and made me sleep on the floor. Cinder is very, very angry.
—Elaine

Entry 4
Today was a good day at school. We made a bunch of snowflakes out of white paper, and I got to bring mine home. I didn't show them to Momma and Daddy. They're hidden under my bed. The kids at school are really excited about Christmas, but Momma says that Santa doesn't give presents to the bad kids, so I don't really have anything to be excited about. She laughed at me when she said that. That made Cinder really mad again, and she mushed up all the chocolate cake Momma made for her and Daddy for after dinner. I had to clean it though.

Momma always thinks I did it. It took all night. I hope I can stay awake
in school tomorrow.
—Elaine

Detective Eubanks set the journal back down on his table and took a deep
breath. He was already sickened, and he had just begun to read. *Who in the
hell could treat a child that way, especially their own child?* It was almost light,
and despite wanting to know who Cinder was, he couldn't bring himself to
continue. He faded off to sleep on the couch, much too exhausted to make the
trip to his bedroom.

He dreamed of his own childhood and his mother. He could see her standing there, yelling at him, and calling him worthless like his father. He was only
six when he walked out on them for another woman, and it had made his life
hell. His mother developed lung cancer soon after, and he solely took care of
her when she became dependent on him—even though she'd always treated
him awful, telling him how he would never amount to anything in the world,
doomed to be a loser like his deadbeat father, who was nothing more than an
alcoholic gambler who couldn't keep it in his pants. Still, he loved her despite
everything. She was his mother, after all, and he did his best to be a good son
no matter how bitter and terrible she could be.

She'd finally lost the uphill battle when he was twelve. His father came back
into town when he heard the news—with a new wife and her two children in
tow—wanting him to move in with them. He really didn't want to, but he wasn't
an adult yet and was forced to go with them. His father bounced from one job
to the next, and his stepmother worked as a housekeeper. With a full-time job,
three kids, and a husband who couldn't hold down a job, she was often tired,
but she did try her best to be there when she was needed.

He didn't need her very often. He was a rather independent boy, doing his
own laundry and fixing dinner for his stepsisters when she worked late, which
was often. His father was typically off drinking and gambling away her money.
When he was sixteen, his father was shot when he tried to cheat the wrong
people in a card game. He wasn't exactly sad to see him go.

Shannon asked David to stay there with her and the girls, which he did until
he turned eighteen. He signed up for the police academy, and Shannon and the
girls went his graduation ceremony.

A few months later, she told him she had found someone. She and the girls were moving to Canada to be with him. He was a software designer who made decent money, and he was glad this man was so good to her and the girls. He stayed in touch with all of them, getting cards each year on Christmas and his birthday. The girls always wanted to know when he was planning on coming up for a visit. They wouldn't stop hugging him at the airport. Shannon planted enough kisses on his cheek to last a lifetime.

The happy visions of his family faded, replaced with something cold and sinister. The smell was horrific, derived mainly of urine. The scent turned his gut, and he felt like he might choke on it. The more he tried to get away from the odor, the stronger it got. He was engulfed in it. He rolled and tossed on the couch, chilled to the bone at the feeling of eyes on him. He felt a tightness around his throat that grew in intensity until small red spots peppered his vision.

He felt as if he might die and thrashed frantically before the feeling disappeared as quickly as it had begun. His breath flooded back, causing him to cough violently. His hand flew out to yank the cord on his lamp. In the empty room, he saw a silhouette at the window. He pegged it as a trick of the light as he caught his breath.

He looked down at his bleeding hand. The stitches had torn open and cursed under his breath. "Dammit," he growled before rubbing his throat with his clean hand. He went into the bathroom, redressed the bandage on his arm, and turned on every light—something he hadn't done since he was a child.

Mealtime at Willow Tree was generally quite noisy, but everyone was drained of all joy. Sarah was trying to shake off the bad feelings. She sat at a table with Joan and Phoebe and was still quite upset with Miles. Nothing made sense to her. She didn't understand how he could make her the most beautiful present ever and then turn around and destroy her precious Tobbie. She shook her head, trying to forget the look on his face when Carrie handed Tobbie to her.

Sarah picked up the plate of syrupy pancakes she'd gotten for Phoebe and started to feed her small bites. She looked over at the empty seat next to Joan that Miles would usually occupy and furrowed her brow. *Good*, she thought.

You just stay in your room while we all eat. You can eat alone, you big stupid. Sarah wiped Phoebe's face where she had let syrup drip down while she was thinking about stupid Miles.

Joan watched Sarah feed Phoebe and remained quiet. She just couldn't believe that Miles had done such a terrible thing to Sarah of all people. There wasn't anybody in the entire building who would have done such a horrible thing—except maybe Kyle.

Sarah was absolutely devastated when she found out where Tobbie had been stashed. She hoped it would blow over so she and Miles would patch things up, but she knew that was wishful thinking after such a horrible thing. There was enough weirdness going on, and the last thing anyone needed was for them to all start turning on each other.

CHAPTER 15

arrie had gone into work an hour early. She wanted to sit in with Elaine before her shift. Dr. Katz was finishing up his examination when she came in. "Morning, Carrie. How are you today?"

"I'm doing all right enough, Dr. Katz, though my mind was on Sarah the whole night." She took a seat next to Elaine.

"Mine too," he said quietly. Carrie looked down at Elaine and reached out to stroke her hair gently. "She just looks so peaceful—like she just is taking a nap," she said.

The doctor smiled, but he wondered if she would feel that when if she woke up to find that things were not the way they should be—and that many people were acting out of character.

"I wasn't going to tell anyone this yet, but Elaine is starting to move. She is responding to stimuli, and her vitals are getting stronger. I feel like she'll be ready to wake up soon." She smiled. "Before the party yesterday, when I was in here, she squeezed my hand twice. I was going to tell everyone, but it was Sarah's day."

"I think it's best to keep this to ourselves. I got a message from that detective. He said he would be here today. He went out to see Elaine's mother and has something he thought I would be interested in seeing. I don't want him to know about her progress. The last thing she needs is that guy bothering her with a million and one questions and accusations, possibly setting back her recovery."

"He went to see her mother?" Carrie's face soured at the thought. "That woman is the one who needs to be locked up."

"I thought you might like the join us," the doctor said, "I know how close you are to Elaine, and I thought you'd be interested in whatever he has to show me."

She smiled and nodded once. "I would like that very much. Thank you for including me in this."

"I trust you, Carrie. You and I both only want what's in Elaine's best interest. Before he gets here, I'm going to get started in on my paperwork. I've gotten a little behind under the circumstances. I will see you later today."

After he left, Carrie decided to go see Sarah and the others, hoping that things were just a little bit better today. She also hoped that Miles and Sarah could work through whatever was happening between them. Gabrielle had taken Tobbie home and assured Sarah that she could fix him.

Detective Eubanks rolled over and looked at the clock: nearly eleven o'clock. He leaped out of bed and threw on a pair of gray slacks, a white shirt, and a striped tie. After he put on his black "cop shoes," a nickname his sister had given, he strapped on his firearm and threw on his coat. He grabbed the journal and bolted out the door. He combed back his hair and used his electric razor to shave at the red lights, glancing in the rearview mirror at the red mark across his neck. He felt a chill before pulling his eyes away and stopping in at Maggie's Coffee Shop for a black coffee and something sweet.

He'd known Maggie for years, and she had his coffee and a hot sugar doughnut waiting for him every day. There was never any charge—just a smile as she told him to just keep her fine city safe and he would be in coffee and doughnuts for life. She'd give him a hearty laugh before going on about how he was the grandson she'd never had.

He chugged down his coffee and was stuffing the last of his doughnut in his mouth as he arrived at Willow Tree. He picked up Elaine's journal and had the unsettling feeling of being watched again. He stopped at the door when he caught the faint smell of urine around him and swallowed, the memory of last night's vivid dream fresh in his mind. He quickly shook his head when he realized he was freaking himself out. *Easy there—it was just a bad night.* He shrugged it off and walked through the doors. While he waited to be buzzed in, there was a looming feeling of unseen eyes, watching and waiting.

Miles grinned as he stepped away from his window, preparing for his encounter with the detective. Today, he would be set free.

Detective Eubanks went up to the third floor. After finding no one at the nurse's station, he continued down to the dining hall.

Carrie smiled and waved him over. At first, he was hesitant, but after a deep breath, he walked over.

"Hello, Detective," she said with a smile. "How are you feeling today?" She pointed to his arm.

"Hello. It isn't too bad anymore. Doesn't hurt nearly as bad as it did."

"That's good. Dr. Katz told me you'd be here today. I'd like you to meet Sarah, and you already know Joan and Phoebe. She's sitting by the window."

Carrie and Joan watched in amusement as Sarah stopped in front of him, getting onto her tiptoes and squinting up at him. "So, you're the one Phoebe bit, huh?"

"Well … yeah, that's me," he replied.

"So what'd you do to her?"

"I didn't do anything."

Sarah sighed and shrugged. "Well, you musta done something 'cuz Phoebe's sweet. She doesn't go around biting people."

Detective Eubanks looked over at Carrie, but she was enjoying the show far too much and grinned at him with a chuckle. "Has she ever bitten you, Sarah?"

"Nope. Of course not, silly. Phoebe's harmless. Are you here to see Dr. Katz? Are you going to talk to him about your problems? He's a great listener. He's great at helping people with their problems."

Carrie came over and said, "Sarah, dear, let's be nice. The detective is only trying to do his job, okay?"

He was rather surprised at this, having been under the impression she wasn't going to be in the least bit compliant with his investigation.

"Detective, shall we go see Dr. Katz? I'm sure he's ready for us." She smiled and started toward his office.

"What do you mean ready for us?"

"I hope you don't mind, but I was asked to sit in on your meeting."

He shrugged, and they walked the rest of the way in silence.

Dr. Katz was sitting at his desk, finishing up on the last of his paperwork. "Ah, Carrie, Detective, please come in and take a seat. You have perfect timing."

They sat in the matching chairs in front of his desk. "Detective, what is it that you've brought with you that you think I might take an interest in?"

Detective Eubanks reached into his coat and passed the journal to the doctor. "It's a journal that Elaine kept when she was a small child. I found it tucked away in her closet at her parents' home."

Carrie passed the detective a rather surprised look. "Did her mother give you permission to take this?"

"No, but I obtained permission to enter her room and found it hidden in a box along with something else I wasn't able to bring with me that's just as disturbing as what I found in that notebook."

"You read her journal?" the doctor asked.

"Yes, I thought it necessary to obtain any information I could about her past that could aid me in my case. I thought it would answer some questions I'd had about Elaine."

Carrie growled. "Those were Elaine's personal thoughts, and you violated her privacy. You had no right to do that to her. Maybe there were things in there that she didn't want anyone to know about."

"I only read it because there were things I needed to find out about her past. Trust me, I didn't get any kind of enjoyment out of reading that journal and robbing her of her privacy. I will probably have nightmares for the rest of my life."

Dr. Katz said, "Detective, did you learn anything that would be beneficial to us?"

"After I read a portion of the journal, I confronted her mother. I expected her to deny everything, but she admitted all of it wholeheartedly: locking Elaine in a metal cabinet for hours on end, sometimes without food, and forcing her to use it as her bathroom when she was trapped in there."

Carrie covered her mouth, and Dr. Katz shut his eyes. A moment later, he opened his eyes and looked back over at the detective. "You said you found something that you couldn't bring back with you?"

"Yes—in the back of her closet. It took some working with the penlight to get a good look, as it was deep in there, but there was some kind of drawing. It looked like a young girl, but her hair was clearly messed up, with big black eyes and pointed teeth. At first, I thought she had some kind of red something in her mouth that might me her tongue, but I found a small drawing of her tongue severed and on the ground by her feet. I discerned that it had been cut out, and she was bleeding from the mouth."

"So she drew a creepy picture on a wall. Lots of kids do that, especially if they're troubled," Carrie said.

"I got a really bad vibe from that drawing when I saw it, and in her journal, she continuously references someone by the name of Cinder, blaming her for everything her mother punished her for. It leads me to believe that she split off some sort of personality, which would explain why she doesn't remember killing Bryce Freeman."

Carrie was tapping her foot on the ground rapidly. "Detective Eubanks, I am positive that if Elaine exhibited split personalities, then she would have showed signs of it immediately when she was sent in, but she's been a perfect patient—and not once has she mentioned anything of the sort that pertains to Cinders or drawings or whatever the hell you keep insisting is wrong with her."

"Would you honestly tell me if you had seen something like that? You seem hell bent on trying to protect this woman for some reason. What hold does she have on you? As a matter of fact, I am quite sure you still haven't told me everything about the night Kyle was murdered! You slimy, no good son of a—"

"Carrie, Detective." The doctor interrupted sternly. "That will be quite enough from the both of you. None of this bickering is helpful in the slightest. Detective, I can assure you we have told you everything we know and are co-operating in every way we can."

"Dr. Katz, this case keeps getting more and more bizarre. I've got the Dunmore family breathin' down my neck. I need to be able to tell them who killed their son. They deserve closure. The only person who was in that room was Elaine, and I need to know what happened."

"Perhaps Elaine may have mentioned Cinder to someone else. Maybe we should ask around." Carrie sat up. "That way, it wouldn't interfere with confidentiality."

The detective said, "All right. Who do I talk to first?"

"No offense, Detective, but I think they will feel better talking to me. I'll ask around—if there's no objections," Carrie said.

"As long as I get to sit in and listen, that's fine by me," the detective said.

"As long as you don't do anything to interfere or upset the patients

They went to the crafts room. Sarah was helping Phoebe paint a popsicle-stick flower, and Joan was painting on a canvas by the window. They walked over to Joan first.

"Sorry to bother you when you're painting Joan, but may we have a word?" Carrie asked.

"Sure." Joan lowered her brush and turned to look at them.

"I was wondering if Elaine ever mentioned anyone by the name of Cinder. I would hate to betray the trust of your conversation, but I wouldn't ask if it wasn't incredibly important."

Joan scrunched her face in thought. "Cinder? Um … no. She's never mentioned anything or anyone by that name. She didn't like talking about her past. She told stories about her trips after she turned eighteen, but nothing before then—if that's what you're looking for. Sorry I couldn't be of more help."

"No. You're fine. You did what you could. I can't wait to see what your new work looks like when it's done. Thank you for your time."

Sarah helped Phoebe hold the paintbrush so she could paint. She seemed considerably drugged up until she turned to look directly at him.

He swallowed nervously and subconsciously rubbed his bandaged arm. He felt a sinking feeling in the pit of his stomach, remembering her teeth sunk in his arm.

She then smiled shyly at him. He smiled back, or at least attempted to, but it came off as more if a grimace.

"Don't worry, Detective," the doctor said. "She's heavily sedated. She's not going to bite you. Poor thing, though, not being able to hold your own paintbrush. It's dehumanizing."

"Are you sure? I swear she just looked at me."

"Yes, I am sure. She physically does not have the ability to hurt you."

The detective took a step away. "No offense, but I think I'll keep my distance if it's all the same to you."

Carrie locked her arm around his good one and led him toward her. "Come on now, Detective. If you face your fears, they aren't really all that scary in the first place—besides, we need to check on Sarah too."

Miles squealed with delight in his room, practically foaming at the mouth and chanting, "It's time. It's time. No more pain." He caught a glimpse of himself in the mirror and smiled a jagged- toothed grin before he swirled the fresh mouthful of blood from his tongue and spit it out on the floor, wiping the corner of his mouth before he headed out of his room.

"Sarah, could you please tell us if Elaine ever mentioned anyone named Cinder."

Her nose crinkled up. "Cinder? What kind of a name is that?"

"I know it's a funny name, but have you ever heard it before?"

Sarah was silent for a moment before clicking her tongue. It was testing the detective's patience and uncomfortable mood to be so close to Phoebe. "Nope, never heard the name before just now." She shook her head before smiling like she'd just said something miraculous.

Phoebe's small voice fell upon their ears as she looked up at the detective. "Cinder."

Carrie knelt down in front of Phoebe. "Have you heard that name before, Phoebe?"

"Cinder," she hissed quietly before putting a finger to her lips. "Shh."

The detective said, "She's just repeating the words she's hearing. I don't think she understands."

CHAPTER 16

"Phoebe, do you know who Cinder is?" Carrie asked.

Phoebe glanced past her and pointed over her shoulder.

Miles was standing in the doorway, looking more exhausted and ragged than she'd ever seen him.

"No, sweetie. That's Miles, remember?" Sarah took a step back.

"Cinder there," Phoebe whispered.

Carrie shook her head. "No, you must be confused, Phoebe. See? That's Miles

Dr. Katz said, "She seems out of sorts. Maybe some rest is in order—and then maybe she could answer your questions." He waved to Nurse Paula, and she crossed in front of the doorway to make her way to Phoebe.

Sarah shrieked out when Miles suddenly grabbed Paula from behind, pressing a scalpel to her throat. "Make one fucking sound, and I will cut your throat, you stupid bitch!"

"Miles," Dr. Katz said as calmly as he could. "Look, you don't want to do this. Whatever's wrong, we can talk—"

"Shut up! Everybody! Shut the fuck up! I don't want to talk. I'm gonna slit her throat, and then it's everyone else's turn. I'll gut you all like the pigs you are!"

The detective's hand crept slowly toward the inside of his jacket.

Miles's eyes darted to his hand as he jerked the scalpel closer to Paula's neck, making her yelp. "I wouldn't do that, Detective," he hissed.

The detective lifted his hands and took a small step forward. "Hey, listen.

Miles, right? Just take it easy. You don't want to hurt her. You're just upset about something. If you talk to us about it, I am positive there's some other way to work all this out."

A small trickle of blood ran down Paula's neck as the scalpel broke her skin. Miles's hand was trembling.

"Miles, please let her go," Carrie said. "We only want to help you—you know that."

Miles ignored her, keeping his focus on the detective.

"Miles," the detective started again. "There's no place to go. Why don't you just let her go, and then we can talk. I know you're going through something, but we really want to help you."

"What the fuck do you know?" Miles snapped. "You don't know me. But I know you, Detective!"

Phoebe started to giggle, causing the women in the room to look at her in confusion.

"Okay, okay," the detective said. "I don't know you, but from what I have heard, you're a very nice guy. I know you don't want to hurt Paula."

"Tell me, Detective. Did you have someone to talk to while you were stuck wiping mommy's ass—or when she told you she hated you?" Miles let out a deep laugh.

The detective tried to hold in his shock. *How the hell could he know about my mother?* He had never discussed it with anyone in the facility. He needed to remain focused so that he could make sure the nurse and everyone else was safe through this.

Sarah took short, shaky steps toward Miles. She was crying, but she tried her best to stifle it. She wanted be strong like Elaine had taught her to be. "Miles, please don't do this. I'm so sorry I got mad at you. I should have believed you when you said you didn't do it," she whimpered.

Miles's eyes shifted from the detective to her, his hand lowering just barely. His lower lip quivered.

"It'll be okay, Miles. I love you, and I don't want anyone to be hurt." She held out her arm and sniffled. "Please let her go and come here. It's all right."

Miles's voice shook as he said, "Sarah, I'm so sorry. Please forgive me. I never meant to hurt anyone." The tension in the room began to decline as the others thought she was going to talk him down from his hold on Paula.

Sarah reached out to take Paula's hand and move her away, but Miles began to gag violently. He jerked backward—with Paula—and his head snapped to the side. A series of crackles went through his bones before his head hung and his eyes focused piercingly on the detective. Without breaking eye contact with the detective, he began to slice Paula's throat.

The detective had no choice. He produced the gun and sent a round flying into Miles's forehead. His body jerked, and screams rang out as Paula fell on top of Miles.

Sarah screamed and scrambled to Miles's side, pushing Paula away. Sarah begged Miles to wake and shook him frantically.

Joan and Carrie tried to pry her away, sending her into a fit until she was free of their grasp. She screamed in agony and cradled his bloodied head on her lap.

Everything moved in slow motion for the detective. His heartbeat nearly deafened him. He'd had to pull his firearm during tense situations before, but he'd never actually had to fire it.

"Detective?" the doctor said. "This has to be called in. Should I do it?"

The detective shook his head and produced his cellphone.

Sarah refused to let go of Miles.

Carrie and Joan were doing everything they could, and the other staff members moved the other patients out of the room.

After the call, the detective placed his phone on the floor.

Carrie offered him a comforting look, though it did little good.

Sarah looked over at him and said, "You! You killed him! Why did you do that? He wouldn't have hurt her—he wouldn't have! I hate you! I hate you! I hate you!"

"Sarah, sweetie, that's enough. He had no choice. It wasn't his fault," Joan said softly.

Dr. Katz told Sarah that it was time to go, but she was having none of it. "Sarah, listen to me. I know that you cared deeply for Miles, but he's gone. We can't change that, and we have to get you cleaned up, okay? There is nothing more we can do for him."

Sarah leaned down and kissed Miles sweetly on the lips. She stood and hugged Dr. Katz.

"I know, dear. This is a terrible thing that happened, but you need to try to stay calm. You know that Miles would not want you to be upset. Why don't you go with Gabrielle and get washed up?"

Gabrielle came over and held Sarah tightly before leading her off down the hall. "Let's go, darlin'. You just come with Miss Gabrielle, and we'll get you cleaned up."

Sarah took one final look at Miles before shuffling out of the room with her head down.

Joan got a hug from Carrie before she left.

Dr. Katz threw a sheet over Miles.

Carrie looked back over to the detective. "How ya holding up?" she asked softly.

He looked at her with bloodshot eyes. "I didn't want to do that. I've never actually killed anybody before."

She put her arm around his shoulder and rubbed his arm comfortingly. "You had no choice. You know that. You tried to talk to him, but he wasn't thinking clearly. Please don't blame yourself. Sarah is just hurting. She isn't like other people. She doesn't understand."

The detective looked at Carrie, and she pulled him into a hug, holding him as the sound of sirens crept toward the hospital. She stayed against him to comfort them both.

CHAPTER 17

Detective Eubanks spent some time talking to his captain, who rushed over to the scene when he got word that he had been involved. He handed over his weapon to Captain Gray, gave him an overview of what had happened, and scheduled an appointment with their station's psychologist for the following afternoon, which was mandatory when an officer was involved in a shooting to determine if he or she are still of sound mind and able to continue in the field. The police were there for hours before Miles's body was finally removed and all the statements were taken down. The patients had gotten restless with so many strangers crowding the facility.

Phoebe sat through mealtime without eating. She was whispering and giggling to herself, but everyone else was far too upset to pay her any mind.

After Sarah had been cleaned up, she wanted to be with Joan. They sat on the couch with Sarah's head in Joan's lap; a mild sedative made her rather lethargic. Dr. Katz had given her permission to stay the night in Joan's room. When they decided to call it a night, an orderly helped Joan walk Sarah down to their room.

Carrie gave a cup of coffee to Detective Eubanks and warned him about how hot it was. "Sorry if it's not the way you like it. I didn't know how you took it."

He smiled weakly and said, "No, thank you. Black is fine."

"Detective, are you going to be all right?"

He looked up at her for a moment. Her eyes were red and puffy. He smiled gently to her. "I'll manage, but how about you? If you're finished with your statement, you should really head home and get some rest. You look like you're about to faint from exhaustion. I'm sure you could use it."

She nodded and smiled weakly. "I will. I just wanted to make sure that everyone was doing all right, including you, Detective."

"I appreciate the concern, but I'll be all right. I just need a cold beer and a good night's sleep," he replied. "Since I'm finished here, how about I walk you to your car?" he added.

"Why not? Let's go," she said.

As they headed toward the elevator, Dr. Katz gave the pair a curious look. He wanted to stay a bit longer to make sure all the officers had left and everything was quiet again—at least for the rest of the night.

Carrie and Eubanks walked out into the parking lot. Carrie had parked two cars away from him, and she turned to face him as they walked up to her door. "Thank you for walking me to my car. I really appreciate the company."

"Don't mention it. Do you have a long drive?" he asked, shifting slightly.

"No, it's only twenty minutes up the road—a little condo over in Briarwood," she said.

"Well, you have a safe drive home. Thanks for … well, thanks for everything,"

She nodded to him. "You're very welcome, Detective. Have a nice night." Carrie opened her purse and began digging through it for her keys. She lost her hold on it, and it tumbled to the ground, spilling its contents onto the cement. "Oh shit, dammit. Dammit. Dammit."

He kneeled down to help her, moving to hand her what he assumed was some kind of compact before she dropped everything and burst into tears. His eyes widened, and he pulled her to him, helping her off of the ground. "Hey now, it's all right. I'll help you pick it all up. Don't worry," he said softly.

"It's not the damn purse. It's just … everything. All this shit keeps happening, and I don't understand any of it. I don't know how much more if this I can take. First, it's all of this strange stuff with Kyle—and now Miles? He's never acted like that, ever! When will things ever be normal again?"

He held her tightly and stroked her head. "Shh, its okay. I promise that things will get better. Come on. You're in no condition to drive. Let me give you a ride."

She nodded and wiped at her face, moving to reach for her purse before he swooped in and picked everything up for her. He dumped it into her bag and helped her into his car.

His head jerked up to look around with the uneasy feeling of being watched, but no one was there. He shook it off and got into the car, driving off quickly.

Dr. Katz sat in his office, feeling as though he'd just aged at least ten years. He called his wife, his rock of twenty-five years. They had three beautiful daughters; two were married with children, and the youngest was twenty-one. She was in the Peace Corps and working on a two-year contract in Kenya. He wanted so badly to be at home, sitting by the fire in his favorite winged-back chair, watching the fire, enjoying a glass of Irish whiskey, and talking to Martha about that trip to Aruba they'd always planned on taking.

Perhaps after this mess was figured out—and he hoped there would be an end to it—he would surprise Martha with tickets. Perhaps it was time to take some personal days. He needed to clear his head and sit on a sandy beach where Martha could relax under a big umbrella and read a trashy dime-store romance novel. He heaved a sigh as he returned to the reality of his situation—and the dread of having to call Miles's family to inform them of his departure from this world.

At twelve thirty, he called the Burgdorph residence. The phone rang three times, and when he had moved to hang up, a young man's groggy voice answered, "Hello?"

"Hello, this is Dr. Katz. I am sorry to be calling at this hour, but I was hoping to speak to Mrs. or Mr. Burgdorph."

"I'm sorry. They're out of the country for another two weeks, but I am their son. Is there something I can help you with?"

"I really should discuss it with them. Is there any way to get into contact with them?"

"Dr. Katz? I know you! You're the doctor at Willow Tree. Is it Miles? Has something happened?"

Dr. Katz's heart sank. "I'm very sorry, but I really must speak with your parents about it. If you could just pass my message along—"

"Please know that no matter what my parents think of what he's done, I did love him—and I let him down by not visiting him or at least writing a letter," Jeff said.

"Miles spoke of you often—with high regard and great pride—if that helps you any, son."

"I know something bad has happened. I will get the message to my parents immediately. Thank you for calling, Doctor."

Dr. Katz gently put his phone on the receiver and sighed to himself, finding no sense in driving home, getting three hours of sleep, the driving all the way back in to work. Martha understood how his job could be, and he found her truly wonderful for it.

CHAPTER 18

avid pulled up to Carrie's home, shifted the car into park, and leaned back in his seat. "Here," he reached down and popped his seatbelt. "Let me walk you inside."

She waved a hand and unbuckled her own seatbelt. "Oh, don't worry. I'll be fine. It's really not necessary."

"I'm not asking. Come on. I want to make sure you get inside all right." He climbed out of the car, opened the door for her, and took her gently by the arm.

Carrie parted her lips to protest, but having him this close was a great comfort to her. It made her feel safe—not that she got scared too easily—but having him beside her made her feel better.

When they climbed the steps and got to the door, he took her key from her and turned it in the lock, pushing her door open. "Come on. Let's get you inside," he said, turning his head to smile at her.

"I appreciate you going through all the trouble of taking me home, but I do think I can take it from here," she said with a chuckle. Despite her words, she didn't really want him to go quite yet, but she wasn't about to let him on to that fact.

His eyes caught the face of a slobbery, growling basset hound as he tilted his head up at him and trotted over on his fat little legs. "Whoa."

"Moe!" She put her hands on her knees, directing her attention down at the beast. "Easy, boy. He isn't hurting me. Relax, baby. Oh, look at you. You're a good boy. Yes, yes you are."

David took a long breath and let it go when Moe cocked his head and returned his attention to him, wagging his tail.

"You could have told me you had a vicious beast in here," he said with a weak smile, brushing off the temporary fear of the dog.

"Moe?" She hung her coat with a chuckle, looking over her shoulder at him. "He's harmless, and besides, the look on your face was absolutely priceless. Made me wish I had a camera when you thought a big attack dog was ready to just tear you up. Pretty funny I think."

"Oh yeah, Hadler, real nice one." He tried not to crack a smile.

There were a few seconds of extended silence, throwing the room into an awkward atmosphere, making Carrie rather nervous. She felt like she was sixteen again, and Danny Futterman was standing on her parents' front porch, getting ready to kiss her—and they did. Their braces got locked together, and her dad had to get them apart again. It was mortifying.

David had read the tension in the room, and butterflies were kicking up in his stomach. He knew the feelings could cause a problem—with her being involved in the murder investigation. Without thinking, he closed the space between them and took her into his arms.

The kiss was brief, yet warm. He expected her to pull away and possibly slap him, but she surprised the both of them with the lightest moan.

When they finally parted, they looked at each other in silence before he cleared his throat and smiled. "I don't make a habit of doing things like this, Miss Hadler, but I just had the need to kiss you. Or, if you think it'd be all right, Carrie?"

She laughed. "I do believe it would be all right if you called me Carrie, but what should I be calling you besides *Detective*?"

"You can call me David." He took her by the shoulders and planted a kiss on her cheek, sending goose bumps down her spine.

"You can sit down if you like." She gestured to her couch and disappeared into the kitchen, leaving him to walk around the room, peering over at her backside as she exited. He noted a large amount of photos of two younger girls, one with a striking resemblance to Carrie; the other looked similar, but he failed to find any that were recent.

She came back into the room with two beers. They sat on the couch, and she handed him a beer.

He pointed the neck of his bottle toward the photo on the end table. "That your sister?" he asked before taking a drink.

"Yeah, that's Elizabeth, but I always called her Liza." She sighed lightly and leaned back in her seat, taking a slow sip. "We were inseparable, the best of friends."

He looked between her and the picture once more. "You guys have some kind of falling out?"

"No. She passed away when I was sixteen. She was ten."

"Oh, geez. I'm sorry." He set his beer down on a coaster. "I didn't mean to bring up bad memories."

She raised a hand and smiled weakly. "No. You're fine. I like to talk about her. I don't get many chances. My parents had a tough time with her illness, and it just got harder for them after she passed. My parents used to get us everything we liked. We had a huge house—big enough for us both to have our own rooms—even though we always wanted to share. After she died, I moved into the room down the hall. It wasn't the same, and I found it hard to sleep in there without her."

He took up his drink again and adjusted his posture. "May I ask how she died?"

"She had leukemia. When she was able to be at home, we'd stay up in her room all day. I didn't want to be with my friends. She was the most important thing to me. There were some days that we'd sit up there for hours. I'd read to her. Since she loved poems, I went down to the library and got as many poetry books I could find. We had a full-time nurse, but I refused to leave her side. I'd hold her hand till the medicines kicked in, and then I'd sit in my chair and watch her sleep."

He reached over and took her hand. "Carrie, I'm so sorry. That must have been hell, being that you pretty much had to go through that by yourselves."

"We had each other, but when she died, I was extremely lonely. If it hadn't been for her, I probably wouldn't have pursued a career as a nurse. I accepted the job at Willow Tree because she taught me that I really wanted to care for people—and I want you to know that those people are very dear to my heart."

He nodded and rubbed her hand with his thumb. "I wish I had your caring heart. I guess being a detective for so long has made me cynical. With all the shit I have to see on a daily basis—and the circumstances I'm under constantly—I guess it's just how I am now. But after Kyle's death and now what's happened to Miles, I am left questioning a lot of things. I mean, Miles talked about my mother. How the hell did he even know about her?" He leaned back, raked his fingers through his hair, and closed his eyes. He took a long drink from his beer and said, "What did you really see the night Kyle died? Please tell me."

"David, I really can't explain it. Elaine was clearly unconscious on the floor, and Kyle was strapped down to the bed, shaking and retching. The blood just … appeared." She took a big gulp of her beer and sighed.

He nodded silently, thinking deeply to himself. He wanted to believe this crazy story, and he did believe in her, but he didn't have to capacity to think on it any more that night. He took her beer, setting both drinks on the table, and kissed her cheek before pulling her into his arms.

"If you don't mind it, I'd like to stay here with you tonight. We both really need some sleep, and I don't feel comfortable leaving you here alone tonight."

"I'd like you to stay." She smiled and turned her cheek into his chest.

Within minutes, the two were asleep in each other's embrace.

CHAPTER 19

D r. Katz tossed and turned on his office sofa before getting up to fix himself a strong cup of coffee. On his way to the kitchen, he was shocked to find Elaine painstakingly trying to make her way to his office.

A nurse was desperately trying to get Elaine to go back to her room.

Dr. Katz rushed to her side and caught her arm just as she was about to collapse. "Help me get her into my office!" he shouted.

The nurse helped him get Elaine to the sofa.

"Do you want to explain to me how the hell she is awake and so far from her room?"

"I'm so sorry, Dr. Katz. It happened so very quickly. I'd only turned away and left her be for just a moment to get another blanket and a fresh pair of sheets. She'd soiled the ones she was in. I'm so sorry. I just wanted to get her cleaned up." The poor nurse looked mortified at the thought of getting fired.

He wanted to continue to yell at her, but she was already shaken enough. He took a deep breath and tried to be calm. "Nurse, how long as she been out of her room?"

"No more than a couple of minutes. I was trying to get her to lie down.

Elaine started to speak faintly and hoarsely. "I'm so sorry … it's all my fault. Everything is my fault."

He knelt down. "Elaine, please don't talk. We need you to rest. Let's get you back to your room."

She shook her head in protest.

"Elaine, we can talk more once you've rested. I promise. We're going to get you back to your room, okay?"

She did not protest.

The nurse got a wheelchair, and they helped Elaine into it.

Elaine muttered, "Cinder."

The doctor's blood ran cold, but things were finally starting to make sense. He had been pushing and trying to get her to manifest this second personality. This was why she had always claimed to be innocent: she did not recollect any of her actions. What Elaine had done was not an uncommon thing. Elaine, having been a victim on her parents' abuse, did the only thing she could think of: she made someone to protect her. He snapped out of his thoughts, and the two took Elaine back to her room.

Once in her bed, Elaine looked at the doctor. "Please, I don't want to go back to sleep. There's something I need to tell you."

He took her arm gently and secured it in the restraint.

The nurse secured Elaine's other arm.

The doctor said, "Shh. It's all right. I understand now. I know what's wrong, and I'm going to help you, but you need to get some rest. These restraints are nice and soft—lamb's wool—and won't hurt you at all." He gave her a sedative and instructed the nurse not to leave her side for anything without informing him.

The nurse settled in beside Elaine with a book, not looking up as he began to walk out of the room. "I mean no disrespect, Dr. Katz, but do you think it was necessary to give her that large a dose of sedatives?"

With the mood he was in, he was set to tell her off, but he took a deep breath instead. "Under the circumstances, I believe it was absolutely necessary."

Carrie was sleeping soundly next to David on the couch when her phone rang. She glanced at the clock—eight o'clock—before picking up the phone. "Hello?" she grumbled.

"Sorry to wake you, Carrie, but I had to talk to you." Dr. Katz's voice immediately woke her, and he explained his theory about Elaine's personalities.

Her eyes widened, and she attempted to remain composed.

David was rubbing his eyes and catching bits and pieces of what she said.

"Carrie, I am also going to contact the detective and have him come up," the doctor said.

"I'll be right there," she said. She headed for the bedroom and grabbed a change of clothes.

David followed close behind and said, "And?"

"Elaine's awake. We have to get over there—right now. Dr. Katz has got it into his head that Elaine's got a split personality. You and I both saw what happened. He's trying to rationalize everything." She peeled off her shirt.

His face turned three shades of red, and he turned his eyes away.

"I'm not a modest person. Besides, I'm sure you've seen a bra or two in your days." She chuckled lightly before she was dressed in record time. She yanked on her hiking boots, grabbed her coat, and led him out the door.

CHAPTER 20

Jeff Burgdorph departed from his plane and made his way to the baggage claim, collecting his duffel bag. He only brought one piece of luggage since he wouldn't be staying for very long. He'd gotten in touch with his parents briefly to inform them of his plans.

Originally, they had been quite furious with him. His mother, who was already an emotional roller coaster, pleaded with him to just leave well enough alone. Maybe they could be all right with it and let things be buried and forgotten, but he was going to do right by him and make sure that Miles was able to come home where he belonged.

His father had refused to listen to him and hung up abruptly, but neither of them did anything to change his mind as he headed to the hospital. The weather was taking a turn for the worse. Jeff's attempts to call Dr. Katz were thwarted by the crappy signal that came with the brewing storm, and he decided to surprise the doctor with his presence instead.

For many years, he wondered what Willow Tree was like—and how it treated his brother. He had always hoped it was not too dreadful, but his parents weren't above placing him in mediocre care. They were able to live their lives like Miles never existed. Keeping him away from Jeff was all they really cared about. They were cold and bitter. He was going to have a funeral for his brother—even if he was the only person there. Miles deserved it.

The ride was longer than he'd first imagined it would be, but after what felt like an eternity, the taxi drove around a bend. There stood the long drive that led up to the gated area and a brick wall. Behind it, he knew, was Willow Tree.

Jeff's first impression was that the outside looked like the perfect scene for one of those high-production horror movies. It paired perfectly with the gloom-iness of the sky. The building was rather impressive, but it appeared to have taken its fair share of beatings. It looked at least half a century old.

This was the place that Miles called home, and Jeff wanted to see what he had seen and lived. He passed the cab fare to the driver and departed the yellow automobile. As the taxi pulled away, Jeff was overcome with loneliness and isolation. He expected as much from a place so far away from society—and he understood the problem an asylum would pose in a crowded city if someone were to escape—but those were thoughts for later. Jeff hurriedly proceeded up the steps.

CHAPTER 21

As Dr. Katz waited for Carrie and David, he noted that the weather appeared as though it were going to get particularly unpleasant. He began to worry about the old electrical wiring of the establishment, hoping it would hold up. He knew it was prone to blackouts in severe storms and decided to tell the staff to prepare. He distributed the emergency flashlights in case of a power outage.

When he had finished up at the nurses' station, the elevator door opened.

An unfamiliar young man stepped out, duffel bag draped over his shoulder, and walked toward him.

"Excuse me. My name is Jeff Burgdorph. I was wondering if you could tell me where I might find Dr. Katz? It's about Miles."

The doctor shook his hand and smiled. "Look no further. You've found me. To be honest, I'm a little surprised to see you here."

"Oh, Dr. Katz, it's very nice to meet you. I'm sorry to just show up. My phone wasn't getting any kind of connection with this storm rolling in. None of my calls came through, and as far as me being here, I don't share my parents' feelings that he should be forgotten. I came here to make the arrangements to have my brother brought home for a proper burial."

Jeff looked strikingly similar to Miles—except for the sandy hair that contrasted with Miles's dark hair. "I'm glad you decided to come down. Why don't we have a seat in my office and have a talk."

Carrie and David were in the parking lot. They had been talking all the way there about the best ways to get Elaine the help she needed.

Carrie was convinced that Elaine hadn't committed a single murder, but David was still trying to convince himself otherwise. He knew there was no way Miles would've known about his mother, but if he had to agree with Carrie, it meant admitting that he had been wrong about Elaine the whole time. It would sound crazy if he marched into his boss's office and said, "I've solved the murder, but the murderer wasn't the one in the mental hospital. Get this. It's some sort of monster fabricated from her childhood." He was sure that would go over really well; the victim's parents would throw him a big party for finding the murderer.

He knew that Carrie had quite a few valid points in the argument, but he had no idea what he was going to do until it was done. It scared the living hell out of him; it was almost enough to drive him to an untimely stay at Willow Tree.

Carrie got out of the car and leaned over to look back into the window at David. "It's still not too late to leave me and my car here and let me do this by myself, you know."

"If you're here to do something illegal, it might be a good idea to have a cop on your side—and I'm the only one here."

She smiled warmly. "Thank you, David. I know we're doing the right thing. I'm sure of it."

They marched up to Dr. Katz's office.

"Carrie, Detective Eubanks," the doctor said. "I'm glad you finally made it. I want you to meet Jeff, Miles's younger brother."

David felt uncomfortable seeing the man who looked like he could be Miles's twin. He wished he'd taken the chance Carrie gave him and left before coming up here. He said his hellos as politely as possible.

Dr. Katz excused himself from the room to join them in the hall, shutting the office door behind them.

Unbeknownst to the group of three as they traveled down the hall toward Elaine's room, they were follow by a pair of bloody footprints, tracing along the floor in fleeting view—and disappearing as quickly as an invisible foot was lifted from the ground.

Elaine was groggy but conscious. One of the day nurses was reading to her.

Carrie walked over to Elaine's bedside. "Hey, sweetheart. It's good to see you awake."

Elaine smiled and yawned lightly. "It's good to be awake."

Dr. Katz stepped over to the foot of the bed. "Elaine, Detective Eubanks is here with Carrie to speak with you—if you're up to it."

Elaine peered around Carrie to take a look at the smiling detective and nodded.

"Great," Dr. Katz stated. "I need to step out for a few minutes to finish up with Jeff, but I'll be back shortly."

The nurse took the opportunity to take a restroom break and stretch her legs, leaving her book on the side table.

David shut the door gently, and the three of them were alone—as Carrie preferred.

Carrie sat at the edge of Elaine's bed.

CHAPTER 22

D r. Katz returned to his office just in time for all hell to break loose outside. A loud crackling noise paired with a clap of thunder and sounded as if it were the furious hand of God striking down upon the earth. One of the large trees was struck down by the bolt of wild lightning.

Dr. Katz jumped at the sound, embarrassed to have been startled by the storm. "Sorry to have to run out on you like that, but I had something I needed to discuss with them. Now, where were we?"

With another thunderous roar, the lights flickered—and then everything went dark. Dr. Katz pierced through the abysmal dark with a flashlight. "I'm afraid to say you may be stuck here for a while. We seem to have lost power. I was afraid this might happen. If you don't mind, we really have to get to the television room. The staff has been instructed to gather everyone there if something like this were to happen. The patients feel more at ease when grouped together."

Jeff followed the doctor toward the TV room.

When the lights died, Carrie knew it would be their only chance to get Elaine out of there. "Elaine, you need to listen to me. We don't have much time, honey. I believe that you didn't kill any of these people. It's a long story, but we have your journal. Detective Eubanks went to go see your mother."

The emergency lights came on in the hallway, and the detective stood to the side with a flashlight.

"Elaine," Carrie said. "Elaine, what does Cinder want?"

Elaine looked confused

"Elaine," Carrie continued. "We don't have much time. I know you're tired, but please tell us what Cinder wants. You don't have to keep this secret anymore. Just tell us why she's so angry."

"I need to go home," Elaine started. "I will know everything there. I'm sorry … I'm so sorry. I thought that if I stayed here and never said anything that she would stay hidden and go away."

Carrie and David exchanged a knowing glance. He could tell it was time for them to make their move, which would undoubtedly place them on the other side of the law.

"Elaine, David and I are going to help you end this pain. You're going to go home, okay? But we have to leave, right now." Carrie drew back Elaine's covers, and David helped her to her feet.

Elaine's legs were rubbery and weak.

Down the hallway they went, slowly but surely, and Carrie remained lookout, double-checking each corner and doorway as they arrived at the stairwell.

David shut the door behind them quietly, and they set off on their proverbial jailbreak.

CHAPTER 23

As the patients settled into the TV room, Dr. Katz said, "Jeff, I truly am sorry that you have to ride the storm out with us. I hope you weren't on a very tight schedule."

"Nope," Jeff replied. "There isn't anywhere I have to be."

Dr. Katz smiled before a nurse hurried over.

"Excuse me, Doctor, but we've got a few situations."

"What is it?" he asked.

"Well, Larry has … well, sir, he's taken this opportunity to remove his clothing. He is running around the hospital and hiding from us."

Dr. Katz's face flooded with relief.

"Well, there is another situation. Elaine wasn't in her room when we went to get her—and the detective and Carrie are also missing."

Dr. Katz could feel his blood chill. He had no idea they would attempt to take her out of the hospital. Where the hell would they even take her? "How long ago did somebody notice she was missing?"

Jeff looked alarmed.

"Just a few minutes sir."

"Jeff, please excuse me. There is a pressing matter I must attend to." Dr. Katz sprinted toward Elaine's room, planning out all possible escape routes. He figured the far stairwell was the safest bet and ran down the stairs.

CHAPTER 24

Carrie and David managed to get Elaine down the stairs and out of the building while being pelted with hail of varying sizes. The rain was coming down in sheets, and the whipping wind forced them to yell to each other. Elaine was acting as if she were in a trance.

David pulled up in the car and came around the side to help get Elaine inside.

Dr. Katz flew down the steps and threw the door open.

Carrie shut the door and got Elaine out of the rain as Dr. Katz ran across the drive.

"Carrie, what the hell are you doing? Have you two lost your goddamn minds? You can't take her out of the hospital. She isn't well! This is kidnapping!"

Carrie put herself between him and the car door. "Dr. Katz, please understand that we aren't hurting her! Elaine needs to go home! She didn't kill anyone—and we're going to prove it."

"Carrie, I know you think you're trying to help her, but if you take her out of this hospital, I will have no choice but to turn the both of you in to the authorities. The girl's got a split personality. If you take her out and she hurts someone else, it's going to be on me. Carrie, think about it. It's not too late to come back inside." Dr. Katz reached for the door.

David pulled out a handgun and aimed it at the doctor. "I'm sorry, Doctor, but I can't let you take her out of the car. I have no choice. I'm afraid you're going to have to come with us. Get in the car."

Carrie looked to David and the doctor.

Dr. Katz knew that the detective wouldn't shoot—or at least was thoroughly hoping he wouldn't—but if he were forced into going with them, at least he could watch over Elaine and keep her from hurting anyone. He nodded silently and got into the car.

David lowered his gun.

Carrie said, "What the hell was that about?"

"I don't know, but let's get the hell out of here before I do it again."

They got into the car and tore off down the road. They drove in silence for a few minutes.

Dr. Katz pressed his hand against Elaine's damp forehead. "Carrie, Elaine's absolutely burning up—and she's muttering. Was she doing any of that before you took her out of her room?"

Carrie looked back at them and said, "No. She started acting like that when we got her to the bottom of the stairs. It seemed like she was zoning out. She wasn't warm, and the muttering is new too."

Dr. Katz gave Elaine a worried glance. "Carrie, I think she's having a psychotic break. She needs to be sedated until it's under control. She hasn't been outside in a year, and this little trip—or whatever this is—may be too much for her to handle. What do you even hope to accomplish by taking her back to her parents' home?"

Carrie realized that she actually did not have a solid answer to his question, but she knew she had a force driving her. She knew this was what Elaine needed, and Elaine said this was where they were supposed to go. "Dr. Katz, I'm sorry that we had to do such a drastic thing, but I believe Elaine has something else that may be wrong. I just have this strange feeling that if we take her home, we will know what it is."

Elaine sat up and stared staring out the windshield. "We can't do that. We can't do that."

Dr. Katz was growing even more concerned. He lacked any medications in case she became difficult to manage, and he feared that this would change her. She might never be the same after something so taxing on her mind. She was not prepared for this, and he believed it wasn't right to bring her back. It could cause even more damage, and he might not be able to undo it.

David was gritting his teeth, trying to focus on their conversation and driving in the rain. He narrowed his eyes. He knew he was out of his mind to agree to this, but if they made it to Elaine's house alive—and managed to help her—his future in law enforcement was surely done. Carrie was committed to doing this—even if it meant doing it alone—but he would have been just as worried about her out in this weather. He knew how difficult the house was to find in the best of conditions.

Elaine was getting worse by the minute.

How can this open-and-shut case get so convoluted? Someone is murdered in a room with a mentally ill woman who had murdered before. That is an easy peg—a quick case. I am speeding down the road after stealing her from a mental hospital.

He knew his feelings for Carrie, and they scared the hell out of him. *What will happen after this is over?* He wanted to hold Carrie and shield her from the cruelty of the world, but she would continue no matter what. He was terrified, angry, and confused, but he knew there wasn't anywhere else he'd rather be.

Carrie's heart pounded in her chest. David had informed her that they were still forty minutes away from their destination. She hoped that everyone at the hospital was managing well with the storm and that all was okay. The weather was like the second coming of Christ. Her hands played with the radio until she found a station that offered bits and pieces of the weather report. The static faded in and out; she picked up tornado watches, sightings, and advisories to stay indoors.

David had to swerve around pieces of tree in the road, and the wind picked up.

Carrie shut her eyes tightly, felt the cold tears on her cheeks, and prayed that they would escape this nightmare alive.

CHAPTER 25

Willow Tree still had no power, and it did not look like it would be returning any time soon. Jeff sat at a table with Gabrielle and an orderly. For the most part, everything and everyone remained calm—until the next roaring clap of thunder came around.

Sarah had fallen asleep, and Joan wanted to stretch her legs. She walked over to the table to join the others. "How ya holdin' up, Joan?" Gabrielle asked.

"Oh, it'd take a lot more than this little storm to scare these bones. Just got Sarah to finally shut her eyes. The poor thing heard that Elaine and the others were missing. I tried to put her mind at ease, but that's not an easy thing to do. That girl gets something into her head, and it pretty much sticks there."

"You're right about that." Gabrielle smiled. "Do you want some water? Take a seat with us."

"No, thanks on the water, sweetie, but I will sit with you. Who do we have here with us on this dreary evening?"

"I'm sorry," Gabrielle replied. "I completely forgot. This is Jeff Burgdorph, Miles's younger brother."

Joan shook his hand and lowered her head. "I'm very sorry about Miles. He was a wonderful young man, and I was glad to have the pleasure of spending quite a bit of time with him. I sort of took him as the son I never had the chance to have."

Jeff smiled weakly. "Thank you for your kind words. I'm glad he had people around him like you that cared and were there for him. I feel terrible that I never came around to see him, but my family … well, they are complicated, to say the least."

Joan chuckled lightly. "Most families are, sweetheart, but Miles talked about you with great pride and an abundance of love. Don't worry yourself about whether or not he loved you. He did. He understood why you never came around—and he never held it against you. Don't beat yourself up."

Jeff nodded. "So how long have you worked here at Willow Tree?"

Joan and Gabrielle exchanged a glance and laughed.

Joan said, "No, dear, I don't work here. I'm actually a patient. I'm not afraid to say it. There's no shame in it. There are many people in here for many different reasons, and it's not like you see on TV with everyone sitting around and drooling all over themselves. There are people who need extra help, and there are others who are capable of taking care of themselves to an extent, but we are all a family."

"I'm sorry if I offended you," Jeff muttered.

She waved him off with a grin. "You didn't, Jeff. I can see how I can be mistaken for staff. I'm sort of the mother hen around here."

"So, where do you think Dr. Katz has run off to?" Jeff asked.

"I'm sure he'll be along soon," Joan said. "For now, why don't we get out the cards and try to keep our minds off the weather?"

Gabrielle got up with a smile. "I think that sounds great. I'll go get them."

The announcer on the news was affectionately calling the storm "Armageddon."

David's knuckles were white from gripping the wheel. They were close to the Cooper home, but he was still taking it slowly. He did not want to test their luck with this storm. When they were out of the car, he would feel like they were all safer.

The wind forced Carrie to hold her breath nervously.

Dr. Katz looked over the damage and worried about his wife. If the phones were down, he would be unable to contact her. She thought he was at the hospital, and he knew she hated to be alone in rough weather. He swore to himself that if he got through this, he'd retire and spend the rest of his years doting on her.

David turned down a single-lane road that was surrounded by trees. The trees scraped against the doors and the windows, and the rain had turned the dirt road into a mud pit. The car almost got stuck a handful of times, but he managed to free it each time.

On the driveway up to the Cooper farm, Elaine started to weep.

Dr. Katz held her and promised that no harm could come to her. He was not entirely sure of that, but he did his best to calm her in this extreme situation.

Carrie gasped at the state of the house when the tree line broke away. The place was scary enough to want to leave immediately, and she couldn't imagine how Elaine had stayed there for eighteen years. It looked like it should have been condemned years ago.

David could dimly see the light of a lantern through the window as they pulled up. "Careful. The steps are not very strong. Wait for us on the porch."

Carrie jumped when the front door flew open.

Mary appeared in the doorway and said, "What the hell do you people want? I ain't got nothin' to steal—and strangers aren't welcome!" Her mouth fell open. "Detective, what the hell do you want now? And who the hell are all these people?"

When Elaine lifted her head, Mary looked like she was about to shit a gold brick. "Why the hell did you bring her here?"

Carrie said, "We desperately need to talk with you. Please. My name is Carrie. I work at Willow Tree. And this is Elaine's doctor, Dr. Katz. Please. If you let us in, we will explain everything!"

Mrs. Cooper eyed them all suspiciously. She sighed loudly and moved out of the doorway, letting them enter.

Carrie wanted to cry.

Elaine was still to weak to walk for herself.

After pushing some things onto the floor, Mary sat down across from Elaine and looked at the detective. "Now do you want to hurry up and tell me what the hell all of this is about?"

There was a loud crash, and the doors and cupboards flew open and shut violently.

Elaine looked fearfully at her mother.

David and Carrie exchanged glances.

Dr. Katz heart pounded, and his mouth hung open in shock.

Elaine said, "She's here, Momma. She's here—and she wants to get you now. I'm so sorry, Momma. I tried to keep her away, but it's too late. She's much stronger now!" Elaine shouted.

A horrific shrill cry came out from Elaine's old bedroom.

"Mrs. Cooper, we need to know who Cinder was!" Carrie shouted.

"Why don't you ask Elaine?" Mary yelled. "It was some stupid shit she made up. I don't have the faintest idea."

Carrie's mind went foggy, and she was filled with an overwhelming sorrow. She had a blurry vision of Mary standing over something in a shadow. She couldn't understand it or rationalize why it was happening, but she wanted to grab this woman and jostle her out of existence.

"Momma, please. You have to help me!"

David glanced over at Carrie again. She was silent and had a weird look on her face. *Something isn't right.*

Horrible images ran through Carrie's mind. They were like memories, but none of the terrible things she was experiencing were familiar.

Mrs. Cooper stood up and shouted, "You take that murderous bitch and get the fuck out of my house! Now!"

A crack of lightning and trumpeting thunder startled them all.

Carrie lunged at the woman and grabbed a handful of her filthy muumuu. "You're lying! Tell me what you did here—or I swear I will kill you myself! Do you hear me, you stupid bitch?"

David pried her away and whipped her around.

Mrs. Cooper clutched her chest and appeared to be on the verge of having a stroke.

"What the hell are you doing?" David asked.

She looked up at him. "I saw it! She did something, and she's hiding it! I can't explain it, but I saw it."

David knew she wasn't herself. That look in her eyes was still not right.

Carrie shut her eyes and gritted her teeth, but the images kept coming. She saw Elaine watching her mother in the garden as a young girl. Mary dug a hole, set her shovel aside, placed a small, padlocked box in the hole, and covered it with dirt. When she was finished, she reached out and yanked Elaine's arms. "You listen to me, girl. Don't you ever go digging here—ever! This never happened. If I catch you out here messing around with the garden, you'll be in a hole."

Carrie gently rested a hand on David's arm before kneeling down near Mrs. Cooper. "Why did you bury her there?"

Mary turned white and whispered, "Who? Who told you that?"

Carrie sat up, tilted her head, and grinned wickedly. "The other daughter … the one in the hole."

David looked at the doctor and Elaine, and they were both as confused as he was at this point.

Mrs. Cooper broke down into sobs.

"You can't know anything. It's not possible. No one knew."

Carrie said, "Well, you better hurry the hell up and tell us if any of us want to survive the night."

Elaine caught Mary's eyes and glared at her.

David went to Carrie's side. "Mrs. Cooper, you had another daughter?"

She looked up at him with bloodshot eyes. "Yes. Elaine was not my only child. There were twins. Like I told you before, I never wanted children. I went into labor at three in the morning in one hell of a storm—like this one. There was no getting to the hospital, and I just went down to the basement with some plastic sheeting. I left Wayne sleeping, but when I got down there, the pain made me collapse. I must have yelled for a good half hour before he woke up and came down to me.

"When he got to me, the baby was already coming; he was the one who had to deliver it. Elaine came out just fine after I pushed for a while, but I could just feel it—and he could tell that I wasn't done. The next one … got stuck somehow. She wasn't coming out easy, like Elaine did. I just kept yelling for him to do whatever he had to do to get the damn thing out. He looked around for something to pull it out or pry it free. He went over to his workbench." Mrs. Cooper put her head in her hands and stopped for a minute.

The room was silent except for Elaine sobbing quietly in the doctor's arms.

Carrie wanted to cry, but she knew she had to press for the rest of the story. "What happened next?"

Mrs. Cooper wailed, "Please! I beg you. Don't make me say anymore. It doesn't matter now. There was nothing we could do!"

Elaine sprang to her feet and screamed, "You tell us everything, Momma! What happened? What did you do?"

Mrs. Cooper swallowed and nodded silently. "Wayne … grabbed the oil filter wrench … it was the only thing that had some kind of hook on it, something to get the baby out, but he must have pulled too hard, or in the wrong way, because when she finally came out, her face … her face was so badly damaged. She was so much smaller and weaker than Elaine. She cried so much. When the storm cleared, we left her there and took Elaine to the hospital to document her birth. I was ashamed of the other one. We didn't think she was going to make it in the first place, but she did … and we had to keep her in the basement, our secret."

Elaine wanted to get up and kill her, but she waited to let her finish the story she was owed.

After what felt like an eternity, Mary said, "As Elaine got older, it was harder to keep our secret. One night … when Elaine was about a year and a half old, she must've heard the crying because she was down there holding it when I went to fix the problem. I was so upset … I yanked Elaine back upstairs and locked her up … and … and I took the box cutters … and I took out the other one's tongue. I was tired of her screaming."

Carrie covered her mouth and looked like she might faint. "She was just an infant!"

Elaine whimpered. "Momma, you kept my sister from me?"

Mary shouted, "You don't understand! She was a monster, maimed horrifically. She didn't have oxygen when she was caught in the womb. She was retarded. I needed her hidden!"

"You didn't give either of us a chance! You should have just killed us both!" Elaine screamed. "I tried so hard, and you just wanted to punish someone for your mistakes! Night after night, I prayed to be a good girl, hoping that you and dad would love me, but you just tortured me—and he let it happen! Why? What happened? When did you take her away from me?"

Mary swallowed. "You'd just turned two, and you were learning to talk. I feared that you would get wise and say something to someone at church. I had so much to do that day, and it just kept screaming. You were yelling upstairs and wanting out of your highchair. The laundry was backing up. I couldn't take it. I squeezed her little neck and rolled her up in a blanket when the wiggling stopped. I locked her in the box, put her under the garden, and was rid of it once and for all."

Elaine was reduced to a sobbing mess. She dropped back down into the waiting arms of the doctor.

Carrie turned to David. "We have to get her out of the ground—now! We have to."

He could tell she wasn't going to take a no from him, but the storm was getting worse. One wrong move—and someone could end up injured or dead. He needed to convince her that they needed to go through the proper channels with the authorities once the storm died off. "Carrie, I want to get her too, but we need to wait until it's safer. I'll call the—"

"She's already been down there long enough. If you won't help me, I'll do it myself. I am not leaving that poor baby alone a single second more!" Carrie started toward the door.

David sighed and followed her. "There's a shovel in my trunk."

Dr. Katz stood up and said, "Let me help. I've been wrong about this entire thing. I want to do what I can to make it up to you and Elaine for not believing you."

Carrie nodded to him before they all went out into the storm.

Mrs. Cooper pleaded for them not to go.

The doctor and David got the shovel, a crowbar, and a flashlight from the trunk. They went around the side of the house to meet Carrie and Elaine. They were soaked to the bone and pelted with rain and hail.

Elaine ripped up the flowers and weeds in the spot she was told never to go.

Carrie pulled Elaine aside as the men made quick work of the shallow grave.

It was difficult to keep the hole from flooding. David heard a scrape with his shovel before something came loose.

The box floated up through the muddy water. Dr. Katz plucked it up from the hole and set it gently in front of the girls.

Elaine placed her hands over the box. "You don't have to hurt anyone now. It's all right."

David pried open the lock with the crowbar.

The lid had scratch marks all over it. Everyone realized the mother hadn't killed her before she was locked away and buried. She must have been terrified when she woke up in the box and tried to claw her way out.

Elaine and Carrie were in tears.

David wiped his eyes, lifted the delicate bundle in the dingy blue blanket, and gently pulled it open. The remains of Cinder came into view: a frail and damaged skeleton with scraps of decomposition hanging from the bones.

Elaine took Cinder from his arms and held her close, kissing her forehead. The wind died down, and the rain slowed.

"She needs a proper name," Elaine whispered.

The screen door swung open and slammed against the back porch.

Mrs. Cooper staggered down the steps clutching her chest, and collapsed on the grass.

Dr. Katz rushed over to examine her. He lifted his head to look at Elaine. He didn't have to say anything for her to know. She simply nodded. It was her mother's time, and she could not be happier to see her go.

When the police finally arrived, Dr. Katz managed to get in touch with his wife. He gave her a brief glossing of what happened and promised to explain when he went home. He called the hospital to calm everyone's worries and told them they would be back soon.

The coroner took Cinder and Mrs. Cooper away.

Elaine sat on the back porch and clutched the little blue blanket to her heart.

Carrie left David to finish up with the police. The captain was en route and would surely want one hell of an explanation. Carrie joined Elaine while the chirping of a single bird rang out. "Elaine, I want you to know that I have always thought you were innocent. I knew you'd never hurt anyone."

Elaine set the blanket in her lap and lifted her head. "I know, Carrie. Thank you, but it doesn't matter if I'm innocent or not because no one will believe a crazy girl's ghost story. It's okay though. Willow Tree is where I need to be. It's the first place that's ever really felt like home. I miss everyone there. I'd like to stay. I really would."

Carrie nodded and gently petted the top of her head. "Anything you need, I'll get it done." She stood up and returned to David and Dr. Katz.

On the way back to the hospital, Carrie and Elaine slept. David thought about his family, thinking it was time to go see them finally. He wanted to get away and think for a few weeks, but the thought of leaving Carrie left a pit in his stomach. He was sure that she also needed some time to herself.

This whole experience had humbled him, and life was far too short to lose and neglect the people he cared about. He pulled out his phone and dialed his stepmother. They talked for a good forty minutes. She was thrilled when he announced he was going to go up and visit them, and the girls were absolutely elated when she relayed the news.

Carrie could pick up bits and pieces of his conversation in and out of sleep, and though she had no right to protest, she wished he wouldn't go. They'd only known each other a short time. There were no solid promises made—and he was free to come and go—but Carrie had developed a deep affection for the big idiot. She wasn't sure if he felt the same way, and she once fallen for a man who had turned around and betrayed her with her best friend. She didn't want anyone to get that close anymore—close enough to hurt her so deeply.

Dr. Katz was staring out the window, and Elaine was sleeping against his shoulder. Elaine really was innocent, and he had gone to his wit's end to disprove it. He had no way to prove it to everyone else now that he knew the truth, and it pained him, but his decision to retire remained permanent. It was going to be hard to leave his patients, but he knew they would understand and be all right as long as they kept the family together and had others to talk to. They were much stronger than they realized, and he smiled before closing his eyes and getting his own rest.

Forty minutes later, David pulled up to Willow Tree. There had been cosmetic damage, but it all could be fixed.

Elaine practically beamed at seeing her home and followed everyone inside. They explained as best they could—without any of the weird things. The other patients were told that Elaine's mother was on her deathbed and needed to confess something—so the group had gone out to see her.

Sarah said it sounded like a great horror story.

Joan just hugged the stuffing out of everyone.

Phoebe looking down sadly, sympathizing with the feeling of being locked away all her life.

They decided it was time to get some sleep after finishing up their conversations.

Carrie saw everyone off to bed and was glad David offered her a ride home. She was glad to spend the time alone with him—even for a little while.

Jeff finished up with Dr. Katz and took his leave, but not before putting in a request to come back to visit Sarah. After seeing what his brother had, he wanted to be there for her since he was gone. He promised to write to her, send her pictures, and fly into town for a visit every couple of months, which put her right back up on her cloud.

Carrie and David drove home in silence, and she didn't think he would come in when they arrived. She was surprised when he opened her door. He took her hand and walked her up the steps to her front door, leaning in and kissing her softly and making her toes curl. When she opened her eyes, he said, "Carrie, I want to tell you that I'm leaving for a few weeks to go see my stepfamily up in Canada."

She smiled. "You don't owe me an explanation. I appreciate it, but we haven't known each other that long—and it's not like we're dating or anything."

"I'd like to see more of you when I get back—if that's okay with you? I don't want to leave you now, but I think I need to go see them and clear my mind. Can I call you while I'm there?"

She wanted to jump excitedly and shout that she'd love it, but she smiled warmly instead. "Of course you can. I'd love that."

He kissed her passionately before he pulled away and gently touched her cheek. He turned away and stopped on the steps, peeking over his shoulder. "Don't forget me."

She chuckled. "Not a chance." She cried herself to sleep that night.

Two weeks later, Dr. Katz announced his retirement. The new doctor was in his thirties and had enough passion to fill a trove of hospitals. Dr. Katz knew he was leaving them in good hands.

Sarah took to Dr. Waters quickly. He was an easygoing, hands-on doctor.

Carrie flipped through paperwork at her desk, accepting the new job as head nurse. She knew that she did not want to leave there; the patients needed her—and she needed them much more. She was doing her final evaluation on Joan—who had gone in front of the judge for her annual report. With the help of her friends and family, the judge decided that she was finally ready to be released.

Joan was nervous—and could hardly bear having to leave her girls—but she wanted so badly to see her friends and family. Everyone was elated for Joan. She was surprised when the neighbor she had stabbed testified on her behalf, delivering the final push to the judge.

Carrie signed off on the final sheet and placed the stack neatly in her folder. She looked at her watch and saw that it was time to pick up Elaine. The coroner had finally released the bodies of her mother and sister, and they'd been planning a burial and a small service. Elaine, Dr. Katz, Joan, and Carrie would attend the service before the doctor dropped Joan off at the bus station. Carrie would take Elaine back to Willow Tree.

Elaine was staring out the window, wearing a black turtleneck and a plaid skirt. She noted that she was much more relaxed. Elaine smiled at her and said, "Thanks for everything you've done for me, Carrie. I've never wanted to be close to anyone 'cuz I was afraid of getting hurt, but now that we're at peace, I feel the need to reach out and let people in. I'll cherish who I have.

Carrie hugged Elaine tightly—both of them on the verge of tears—before she pulled back and smiled. "Are you ready to go? They're waiting down at the car."

Elaine nodded, and they headed out.

It had been an emotional morning. All the girls sat with Joan as she prepared to leave.

Sarah cried so hard that Joan had to cradle her and comfort her until she stopped.

Phoebe had made excellent progress and was starting to assert herself and give her opinions.

Sarah still missed Miles, but Jeff had kept his promise. He wrote to her as soon as he got home, sending pictures and promising to visit in a few months.

Joan's ex-husband asked if he could pick her up at the station, which shocked her—but also excited her—since they had not spoken in years. He wanted to spend some time with her if she was okay with it. She'd never stopped loving him, but she wanted to take things slowly. It had been so long since she'd been outside, and the world was different.

As they drove up to the cemetery, Joan held Elaine's hand tightly. "I want you to know that I am going to miss you dearly—and that I am so proud of you. I would have been honored to be your mother."

Elaine looked up at her and wiped her eyes. "You're the closest thing I've ever had to one, Joan. I hope you have a wonderful life outside. I love you."

"I love you too, my sweet girl." She petted her head.

Carrie and Dr. Katz cried in the front seat.

The pastor from Dr. Katz's church gave the service. While planning the service, Elaine told the doctor that she wanted to give her sister a proper name and decided on Mary Katherine Cooper. Carrie thought it sounded beautiful. The service was short and nice. They'd gotten two-dozen white roses and a small casket for her remains—wrapped in a pink satin blanket—and buried with the first and only toy she'd ever have. The little doll had long black hair and a pretty pink dress to match the blanket.

Elaine closed the service with a small prayer, and everyone went to take Joan to the station.

They all said good-bye and returned to the hospital. It had been a long day, and Elaine was eager to get back and write for a while. She found it therapeutic, and Dr. Katz said that it helped her make great progress.

After a few minutes Sarah interrupted her, but Elaine didn't mind. Sarah needed her—and she would drop everything to give her undivided attention.

Sarah waited ten minutes before coming over with a letter. "Elaine! This time, he wrote to me about his school. Apparently, they have all kinds of parties there. People do silly things." She laughed. "He says he wishes I was there, he misses me, and he likes the way I listen to him and don't go on and on about myself."

Elaine put down her notebook and smiled. "Sounds like he really cares for you, Sarah." She chuckled. "I'm really glad for you. I wish you all the best with that, but if he hurts your feelings, you better make sure he knows he's going to be in a world of trouble with me."

Sarah wrapped her arms around Elaine and jumped onto her, knocking them both back on the bed in a fit of giggles. "I'm glad you're back for good, Elaine. I love you."

Elaine smiled and squeezed her. "I love you too, kiddo—and I'm glad to be back. I'll stay right here with you and everyone from now on."

Sarah smiled, bounced off the bed, and ran out of the room. She'd promised to teach Phoebe how to play gin rummy.

Elaine smiled and went back to writing.

Carrie was about to climb into her car when her cell phone went off. She dug it out of her bag quickly in the hopes that it was David. She'd only heard from him once the entire time he was gone. Her hands were shaking, and she was practically holding her breath when she answered.

His familiar voice on the end of the line made her heart skip a beat, plastering a smile on her face. "Carrie, I'm sorry I didn't call you sooner, but there's been something on my mind. I was wondering … well, I want you to know."

Carrie started the engine. If she didn't distract herself, she was going to go mad with his dancing around what he wanted to say.

David chuckled. "I wanted to surprise you, but it seems you aren't home. I was hoping you would be soon. I had to hear your voice."

Her eyes widened as she bolted for home. "Yes. That's wonderful. I'm on my way! Don't you dare move!"

He chuckled. "I'm not going anywhere."

She hung up and sped to him.

David sat with sweaty hands at the bottom of her steps. He had a dozen roses in his lap, and he felt like he might pass out from nerves. All he could think about was Carrie, and he knew that he needed her in his life. His sisters had helped him pick out a ring. The experience they had shared showed him just how passionate Carrie could be about life—and he knew that was something that he needed. He wanted to be her safe place to fall, and he didn't want another day to go by without telling her that he loved her.

When Carrie pulled up, he hid the little box in his pocket and stood.

She scrambled out of her car and ran over to him.

He pulled her to him and felt her melt into him as he kissed her.

She smiled brightly. "First off, these are yours." He handed her the roses.

"Nobody's ever bought me flowers, they're beautiful."

"Carrie, you deserve them every day. I want to be the person you can lean on and feel safe with. I want to be there for you to laugh with or for comfort when you're upset." He dropped to one knee and produced a ring. "What I am trying to say is will you marry me?"

She was absolutely speechless, and joyful tears pressed her cheeks. "Oh, David. Yes! I'll marry you—of course."

He slipped the ring onto her finger, spun her in his arms, and kissed her deeply. "I love you," he whispered.

"I love you too. Now let's go inside and celebrate." She giggled excitedly. "I can't wait to tell everyone!"

Later that night, Elaine thought of how Sarah snored under her breath in the bed beside hers. There was still so much to try to comprehend. She knew a part of her would always feel the guilt of being the one who lived, but the life she had lived was not exactly wonderful. Her parents were not kind people, and they never showed her any love.

She wanted to share her story with the world—to let others know they were not alone. There were people who loved and cared for them. She wanted them to know Mary Katherine and know that she never had a chance to know love. She had contemplated scrapping everything she'd written and starting something completely fresh. This was going to be a book about how—even with a tragic past—anyone can grow into a positive force in the world. Elaine went to bed that night and dreamed of a warm and happy day with her sister.

The next morning, Elaine woke to the sound of Sarah giggling and staring out of the window with a smile. Elaine rolled out of bed and saw at least a dozen butterflies with big, beautiful wings. It was still much too cold for butterflies to be in season, especially in such a large group. Elaine was confused for a moment—until her puzzled look melted into a warm smile. A glow fell over her and the room. She placed her hand gently on the window as each butterfly took to the air, the last staying behind, seeming to peer into the window.

"We're free, Mary Katherine. We're free."